LOVING A REBEL

LINDA FORD

CHAPTER 1

GLORY, MONTANA, SPRING 1884

Flora Kinsley squinted into the blinding snow. Could anything more go wrong on a day that had started out so shining and bright? She was lost, with no idea how far she was from town. Not that it was her fault. She'd ridden hard, certain a rider followed her and gained on her. In her attempt to avoid the man on her trail, she'd pushed her horse too hard and it came up lame. And now a snowstorm.

"Montana, you sure did let me down. Guess I'll be moderating my praise of you in the future." She'd loved the Territory since her family moved west a few months ago. So wild and free. Just as she wished to be.

She'd been warned over and over to moderate her wildness. *You reap what you sow.* The dire words had done nothing to slow her down. Moving to Montana Territory had given her so many exciting opportunities. Riding like a man thrilled her as she raced across the countryside.

She sighed. Seems the predictions of her parents and sisters were about to come true if she didn't soon stumble upon the road to town.

As a preacher's daughter she knew about prayer, and although she generally figured her parents did enough praying that she didn't need to bother, they weren't there at the moment and were unaware of her circumstances. She'd have to do her own praying.

"God, I'm lost, and it's snowing fit to bury me alive. Could You please guide me home? Or at least to shelter. Without the company of that man following me." Though she hadn't seen any sign of him in the last half hour. Maybe he'd watched the storm approaching and found some place to hunker down where he'd be warm and dry.

"Wouldn't mind being warm and dry myself." She spoke aloud to keep her senses clear. Though she wasn't desperate enough to wish to share the same shelter as the man following her. She'd glimpsed enough of him to know he was unkempt and dirty. And the way he kept on her trail made her think he had more in mind than a friendly visit. "I'll freeze to death first." She squinted into the white curtain hoping…praying for something to guide her to safety.

Did she see a light? She narrowed her eyes as the bright patch flickered and disappeared. Swiping the snow from her lashes she stared hard in the direction she'd seen it. Might it be only her imagination? No. There it was again.

"Thanks be to God." She quoted one of her pa's favorite sayings.

But what if it was the man she fled? She approached slowly, prepared to turn and go the other direction if she got so much as a glimpse of him. In a few more steps she thought the light filled a square. Yes. She had stumbled on the dwelling of one of the homesteaders who had moved into the area. The snow flurried around her, blocking her view. Then it swirled away enough for her to make her way to the house.

She banged on the door and shivered as she waited for an answer.

The door opened.

"You," she said. Just when she thought things couldn't get worse. "Kade Thomas?"

"Miss Kinsley, what are you doing out here in the midst of a storm?" His voice rang with displeasure.

She shrugged just as she had when he'd been equally clear about his opinion of her a week ago in town. "My horse is lame. Can I leave him here and borrow yours to get home?"

"Miss Kinsley, take a look around you. We're in the middle of a storm. You can't see two feet in front of you."

"But I must get back to town." Her parents would be distraught if she didn't return soon. "I'm sure I can make it if you will point me in the right direction and allow me to leave my horse here." She looked behind her, to her right and left, hoping for a glimpse of the town of Glory nearby.

"So, you're lost. Your horse is lame and—" He sighed. "Everyone tried to warn you that your rash actions would bring you grief."

She huffed. "I suppose it's my fault a storm has blown in."

He shook his head without answering.

"I know you don't approve of me. You made that very clear already." Her nerves twitched with the memory of last week. She'd gone out riding and lost track of time. In her hurry to get back before her parents would worry, she'd ridden down the alley behind the hotel and right into the midst of some rowdy cowboys. One of them caught her horse. Hands grabbed her, threatening to drag her from the saddle.

That's when Kade had stepped from the shadows. She'd met him before. Ma made a point of inviting the cowboys who attended church to join them for dinner after the service. Kade had come on two occasions. After that, he had refused the invite, saying he must get home.

He had warned the rowdies away and led her horse homeward. As soon as they were away from the others, he'd made his opinion very clear. "A girl with any sense would avoid such situations. I've found those people who have no regard for safety and common sense often end up in trouble. Far too often others also pay the price of their foolishness."

His assessment of her had stung then and still burned beneath her breastbone.

"I know your opinion of me, but does that mean you won't help me?"

With a weary sigh that scraped along her nerves, he stepped aside. "You better come in out of the cold before we both freeze."

"No thank you. Just point me toward town and

I'll be on my way." She'd walk, taking her time so Dollar could favor his leg.

"It's half an hour ride to get to town." He pointed to his right. "On foot, in the snow, it would take much longer and it will be dark before you get there."

"Thank you so much for your help." She let sarcasm color her words and turned toward the direction he'd indicated. But before she took two steps, he reached out and stopped her.

"Gal, you've been in Montana long enough to have learned a little respect for the weather even if you've learned none about wise conduct for yourself." His gaze took in her trousers and no doubt, her hair, which had blown free from the braids she had tamed it in before she left home.

Oh. Her insides flamed. How dare he judge her? Just because she liked the freedom of wearing trousers and riding fast and unfettered.

She yanked free of his hold. "I can look out for myself."

He caught her arm again, holding the sleeve of her coat firmly enough she would have to leave the warm garment behind in order to escape his grasp.

She wasn't that foolish, even if he thought so.

"Kindly unhand me." Her eyes burned with heat.

"No. You can't wander off into a storm. It's not reasonable."

Arggh. If he made one more disparaging comment about her mental abilities, she would not be able to contain her brewing anger.

"What are you suggesting?" Her voice was cold as the snow falling about her shoulders.

"You'll have to stay here until the storm ends."

She gave an unladylike snort. "I'd sooner wait it out in a snowbank." She flung her arm in an arc that forced him to release her and stomped away, shivering with the cold.

Never would she admit that a large dose of fear made her teeth rattle even more than the cold.

* * *

FOR A HEARTBEAT, Kade considered letting the fiery red-haired woman wander into the storm. He had seen enough of her, and heard even more, to know that she flaunted rules and cared nothing for her own safety. Exactly the sort of woman he meant to steer a wide path around. He did not need any more of that kind of aggravation in his life.

But his conscience wouldn't allow her to venture into the storm where she'd surely perish.

He would do the right thing even if he lived to regret it. He stepped into the thickly falling snow and blocked her path. "You cannot leave. I forbid it."

She drew up, and even in the damp cold he felt the heat of her anger. "You forbid it? What makes you think you have that right?"

He swallowed back a sigh. He should know better than to order a rebel to do something...anything. "I'm sorry. But please do not leave. I fear you will perish in the storm. I'll gladly offer you shelter until it's over." And not one minute longer.

She considered his words, glanced past him into the thickening storm, checked to her left, squinting into the snow, then sighed loud and long. "It wouldn't be fair to my horse to make him go further. Very well. Show me to the barn and I will tend him."

"I'll get my coat." He slipped into his shearling-lined denim jacket, lit the lantern, and held it before him as he pulled the door shut. Standing with the house open to the elements had left it cold. Perhaps the room would warm up by the time he got back.

The snow swirled around them as they crossed to the barn. He hung the lantern and, for the first time since he'd opened the door to her knock, looked closely at Flora Kinsley. Her flaming red hair hung about her shoulders, flecked with snow. Snow clung to her dark lashes. She wore trousers just as she had a week ago when he rescued her from some rowdy cowboys. That day he'd seen her safely home to the stables at the back of the churchyard. A few minutes later, she'd emerged wearing a skirt. He couldn't say if she changed inside the stables or pulled the skirt over her trousers. But he did understand that she knew her parents would be shocked to see her attired in men's wear. It gave him cause to wonder what else she did that would shock her parents if they knew. Not that he cared. But he intended to pay heed to the warning in his head that this woman had no thought for her own safety and reputation. Anyone having anything to do with her would suffer from her choices.

She bent over her horse's right front leg and lifted it to check the injury. "Dollar," she said addressing her horse. "The good news is it's just a pebble caught in your hoof." From her pocket she withdrew a jackknife and dug out the pebble. Then she folded the blade away and stuck the knife back in her pocket.

"Are you carrying a pistol?" He'd seen the bulge in her coat.

"I surely am. I'm not so foolish as to ride out on the range without protection."

"And yet foolish enough to ride miles from town with no escort."

She flicked a look at him that said most clearly that she considered his words ridiculous. She glanced around. "Guess I could shelter here. Don't suppose you have any way of securing the door against intruders?"

He studied her long and hard. "Seems a little late to worry about your safety."

She shrugged. "Suppose you're right." As she talked, she removed Dollar's saddle and blanket while he put out some hay for both his horse and hers.

Flora placed her gear on the floor in the corner away from the door and sat down. "I'll be fine. You can leave." She waved him away then pulled off her hat to release more tangled curls about her face.

He saw red—not the color of her hair but the anger coiling inside him—at the arrogance and foolishness of this woman. How did her parents and sisters put up with her? "You aren't staying here. Get up and come to the house with me."

Her dark eyebrows rose. She said nothing nor did she move to obey him.

He rubbed his fist along his forehead. Why was he being so overbearing with her, especially when he knew she'd resist any hint of an order? "What I mean is, you can't stay out here. It's too cold. If you come to the house, it will be warm and I can fix us something to eat." Her eyes flickered with interest.

"Maybe some hot tea or coffee too." He waited, letting her take her time, letting her think she did only what she wanted. In a flash, he saw a reminder of his pa, his brother, Esau, and, Pearl, the girl he'd thought to marry. They, too, hadn't cared about being careful or doing things the rational way. And look how that had turned out.

"Very well." She sprang to her feet and crossed to his side, giving him a look that seemed to say, let's get moving.

He grinned. "In a hurry are you? Hungry, thirsty?"

"And cold." She shivered.

"Come on then." He opened the door to the wind-driven snow. He couldn't see the house, but that wasn't a problem. "Best hang on to me so you don't get blown away. Sure would hate to think of you lost out there." He half expected her to refuse but then she fisted the material of his coat and clung to his back as he led the way.

He pushed into the snow, reached the house, and hurried them into the warmth. It hit him then, just how tiny his place was. Two rooms. A bedroom of sorts, just big enough to hold a narrow cot, and this room, which provided living space. It had seemed adequate and cozy until now, but with Flora here the walls crowded in on him.

He closed the door and rubbed his hands together. "The temperature is really dropping." He hurried to the stove. "Tea or coffee?"

"Tea, if it's all the same to you."

He filled the kettle, hoping he wouldn't have to go outside and pump more water before the storm ended. "I suppose you're hungry." The light was already fading because of the thick snow outside.

"Don't bother on my account." She slipped out of her coat and stood next to him at the stove, her hands outstretched for the warmth. "I hope it lets up soon."

He put a fry pan on the stove. It already held a thick layer of bacon fat. When it began to sizzle, he tossed in a bowl of boiled potatoes and left them to brown. He liked them crispy.

All the while, she stood at the stove watching his every move.

He poured tea, lifted the crispy potatoes out, and added half a dozen eggs. "How do you like yours?"

"Flipped over and no runny white."

He turned each of them with a skill of having spent most of his life doing so. He filled two plates and indicated the nearby table.

She followed him much like a hungry puppy and sat across from him. She grabbed her fork and gave him an expectant look.

He understood what she didn't say...she didn't eat without asking a blessing on the food. He bowed his head and prayed. "Father God, thank you for shelter, safety, and adequate supplies. Amen."

Her smile, fleeting as it was, made him curious.

"What?"

"Short and sweet," she said.

He understood she meant his prayer. "And to the point."

Her eyes sparkled. He'd noticed at their first introduction how blue they were. Like deep mountain lakes or the Montana sky just before dawn.

"It certainly was." She dug in to her food. "This is good."

"Thanks." Silence fell between them.

She glanced toward the window several times. "Doesn't seem to be letting up." Her hands scraped across her knees.

He said what she'd likely been avoiding as much as he had. "It's getting dark. I'm afraid you'll have to spend the night."

Her chair flew back as she jerked to her feet. "That's impossible."

"You're worried about your reputation?"

"No, that's of little concern to me. Ma and Pa are going to worry."

"Don't you think it's a little late to think about how your choices affect them?"

She leaned over the table, gripping the edge hard enough to make her knuckles white as marbles. "It wasn't my choice to make it storm. Don't blame me."

"*Don't blame me.* I've heard that phrase before. But if a person gave their choices a little more consideration, things would be different."

They stared at each other, her eyes flashing like roaring water. His felt full of stubborn accusation. The last thing he needed in his life was another person with little regard for how their choices affected others. And yet here she was. The rebel redheaded Kinsley gal. The preacher's daughter.

He couldn't see her father turning a blind eye to the fact his daughter spent the night with a man, no matter what the circumstances.

There was no way this was going to turn out well.

And just like every other time, he could see the end result but was powerless to stop it.

His food sat like a rock in his stomach.

How did these people manage to make their way into his life?

CHAPTER 2

lora took a deep breath—several of them, in fact. He had no right to make it sound like she'd purposely gotten turned around and lost her way and then brought a storm down about her head. If not for her trying to make it impossible for that man out there to follow her...

She hoped the snow had convinced him to head for shelter and forget about her.

But stuck here overnight? No need to wonder what Ma and Pa would say about that.

Flora clenched her teeth. She grabbed the stack of dirty dishes Kade had piled in front of him and carried them to the cupboard. "Thank you for the meal. I'll wash the dishes."

"Glad I could feed you, but no need to worry about the dishes. I can do them. After all, you're a guest in my house."

She kept her back to him but didn't need to see his face to note the emphasis on the word *guest*. Did he think she was too foolish to even do her share? Despite his opinion of her, she had been raised right. She found the dishpan and poured in hot water. He tried to elbow her aside, but she refused to budge. "I can do my share."

"Fine, I'll dry." He grabbed a towel from the bar behind the stove and took the first plate as she handed it to him.

The air between them was so frigid, it might have followed them inside.

Something he said nagged at her thoughts. She knew if she had a lick of common sense, she would ignore it, but seeing as he thought she didn't have any, she would ask the question.

"You said you've heard the phrase before, *don't blame me*. The way you said it made me think..." What could she say that didn't sound rude? "Well, like you didn't care for the outcome."

"I didn't."

"What happened?" She felt his stiff silence between them. "Never mind. It's of no concern to me." It wasn't like she cared to learn about him.

"Let me just say that on more than one occasion I suffered the consequences of someone taking that stance."

"I'm guessing it must have been someone close to you."

"You could say that."

She waited. And waited.

He dried a plate and put it on the shelf above them and then finally spoke. "Seems to me a person should consider how their choices affect not only themselves but how they impact others."

Her short laugh was half amusement, half mockery. "You and my sister Eve would make a good pair. She's always concerned about doing the right thing and not offending anyone." Her voice grew heated. "How can a person enjoy life if they are striving to please everyone they see? Seems to me people should be living their lives and letting others live theirs. I don't do anything to purposely hurt anyone, but how can a person please everyone? Shouldn't we seek to please God and not man?"

A beat of silence, heavy with her anger and frustration.

He slowly wiped the forks and put them in the tray on the shelf. "I met Eve. She seems steady."

"Steady? Yes, she is, but what a dull word. But don't misunderstand. I love her. She's my sister three times over. I just don't want to be pushed and pulled into what others think I should be."

Kade leaned his hip against the cupboard and stared at Flora. "How can she be your sister three times over?"

Flora chuckled. At least she'd earned a spark of interest from him. She had begun to think he was so stiff and upright he had no interest in anything but rules. "First, we were born sisters. Then we were adopted by the Kinsleys. And third, we are sisters in our belief in Jesus as our Savior."

He studied her. She studied him right back. His hair was the color of mink fur and a tad longish. His eyes were the color of rich soil, carrying the warmth of spring and the promise of good things to come.

She mocked her assessment of him. As Eve would say, she had a wild and vivid imagination.

"So you're adopted?"

"All the Kinsley sisters are."

"All four of you? That sounds like quite a handful."

"Actually, there are six of us sisters. Two stayed back in Verdun, Ohio. Adele is married. Happily, I hope." She had her doubts as to whether or not that was the case but kept her opinion to herself. "She has a little boy. And Tilly is working for a rich family. I think she hopes the son of the family will marry her."

"Marrying well and wisely is important."

She couldn't tell if it was a question or statement and chose to ignore it either way, being quite certain her opinion of what constituted a good marriage would differ vastly from his. If she ever married, it would be to someone who wouldn't try to control her.

He dried the last dish and hung the towel. "I thought you'd have something to say about that."

"No doubt you did." She turned to study the room. "You build this place yourself?"

"Yup. Last year."

"Nice." She wandered from the kitchen area to what she supposed would be the sitting area though it was really one small room. There was a soft chair beside a low bookcase with a Bible sitting on top of the bookshelf. She pointed to the Bible. "Looks new."

"I bought it for my house."

"May I look at it?"

"Of course." He remained in the kitchen area, leaning against the cupboard, his arms crossed.

She studied him a moment. He seemed so distant. So controlled. She dismissed the thoughts and lifted the

Good Book, opening it at the flyleaf. She read aloud, "'This Bible belongs to Kade Thomas and will always have a place of honor in his home.' Hmm. Nice words. Sounds like something Pa would say. And certainly approve of." She returned the book to its place. "Of course, he would add that it needs a place of honor in our hearts."

Kade chuckled, a dry sound as if it wasn't used often enough. "Never thought to hear Flora Kinsley preaching."

His words stung, full of judgment as they were, but she pretended to take no note of them. "Not preaching. Just speaking the truth." For some reason, she felt compelled to add, "Doing things for show is pointless."

He straightened and crossed to look out the window. "I suppose that depends on what you are specifically referring to."

"Guess so." Having no desire to continue this line of conversation, she studied the piece of old wood next to the Bible. "That's an odd decoration." It was obviously from something broken. It was weathered grey with sharp edges sticking out.

"It's a reminder."

She shuddered. "Doesn't look like something one would want to be reminded of."

"It's from the wagon that overturned and killed my father."

Her heart clenched. "I'm so sorry."

"It was a long time ago."

She studied him. "Look at that. We have something in common. I lost my pa when I was a baby."

"I was thirteen."

"That makes it even harder. At least I don't have the memory of losing my pa."

"But you also don't have any good memories of him."

"I know." She turned back to the bookcase lest he guess that tears stung her eyes. "I remember my ma a bit." She shrugged. "I was only four when she passed, so I think mostly what I remember is what Eve tells me. I don't like to think about the past."

"Why not? Seems the past has lots to teach us."

She fingered the dry and cracked leather reins hanging above the bookshelf. "Seems to me it mostly teaches us to live each day to the fullest because we don't know when life will be snatched away."

Kade crossed to the room and slipped the old reins from her hand and pressed them to the wall. "I believe the past teaches us to live wisely so life isn't needlessly snatched away."

"Why do you have old reins hanging here? Shouldn't they be in the barn? Seems odd for someone like you to let these dry out and disintegrate."

"They're a reminder."

"Another one. Were these reins on the horse that pulled the wagon that carried your pa?"

"No. They were on the horse that fell to its death in a ravine and took my brother with him."

Flora jerked her hand away from the bits of leather. "He died?" She couldn't keep the shock from her voice.

"Yes, he did. Needlessly, I might add."

"I'm almost afraid to ask how that could be."

Kade stared at the wall, or more precisely, the reins hanging there. "Esau—that was my brother— entered a crazy race. They had to race across a desert and jump a canyon. The winner got a hundred dollars. I tried to talk Esau out of it. I knew it was dangerous, but he said the money would go a long way toward buying the ranch we had set out hearts on. He didn't make it. His horse missed the far bank of the ravine and both plunged to their death."

Thanks to Flora's vivid imagination, she pictured it all in living color. Felt the shock Kade's brother would experience as he realized he was falling to his death. Saw the battered bodies of the man and horse and felt the horror Kade must have experienced. For a moment her voice wouldn't work. She sniffed. "Kade, that's dreadful." The words quivered from her mouth.

"People shouldn't do foolish things." He jerked about and returned to the window.

Flora stared at the broken piece of wood. She could not look at the reins. She moved her fingers along the bookcase, touching the objects on top—an unlit lamp that he would use for reading, a small mantel clock, the ticking filling the silence of the room. She sank to the soft chair and studied the row of books. Something peeked out of one book. A lacy hankie. She smiled as she pulled it out. "Seems you have a lady friend."

He shook his head.

"It belongs to your mother?"

"Ma died when I was eight. I have nothing of hers. No, it belonged to a girl I meant to marry."

"Meant to." She wasn't sure she wanted to hear his story, but she couldn't let it hang unfinished between them. "She died?"

"Nope. Ran off with someone else."

Flora put the hankie back and stared at the floor. "No

wonder you're so morose. Your life has been full of awfulness."

"But don't you see? It wouldn't be if people had only made wise choices."

Again, she felt his judgement. As if she was personally to blame for the life that had befallen him. "Bad things happen to those who live careful, narrow lives too." She turned back to the display to her left. Mementos of loss. And the Bible beside them. Somehow it didn't fit. "Why do you want to cling to the past when life beckons to be enjoyed today?"

"I'm not 'clinging,' as you call it. But I don't intend to forget the folly of not considering the consequences of one's choices."

She was tired of going around in circles on the subject and went to the window where she rubbed at the glass. "It's dark out." The wind battered the house. Something heavy hit a wall. Her heart slammed into her ribs. She went to her coat where it hung next to the door and yanked her gun out of the pocket.

Had that man followed her here? If so, he'd discover that being female did not make her easy prey.

* * *

A BURST of laughter escaped Kade's mouth, catching him by surprise as he watched the redhead aim her gun at the door. He decided not to point out that she hadn't cocked it, so no one was in danger. "You planning on shooting the wind?" he drawled.

She kept her gaze on the door. "Might be more than the wind. You ever think of that?"

He edged closer, studying the way her eyes darkened and narrowed, noting how her lips pressed together hard. "What are you so afraid of?"

"Who says I'm afraid?"

"Maybe the way your hand shakes. I suggest you put your gun aside before someone gets hurt."

She hesitated then lowered her arm. "Thought I heard something," she mumbled.

"The wind, maybe?"

"Something hit the side of the house. You must have heard it."

He continued to watch her. "You expecting someone?"

She pursed her lips. "Are you suggesting I arranged a rendezvous out here?"

"Did you?"

"Mr. Thomas, I don't even know where *here* is."

The truth of what she said hit him. "You were truly lost?" He'd thought she might have been exaggerating.

Her silence was answer enough.

"You..." He tried to piece together the bits he knew of her predicament. Lost. A lame horse who looked to have been ridden hard. Out late in the afternoon. He understood that she didn't like to worry her parents, so why was she out so late? "Why weren't you watching the weather? Why weren't you paying heed to where you were?"

"I was. I'm not stupid."

Not stupid but—

She interrupted his thoughts. "Nor am I foolish."

"Then explain to me how you got lost."

She returned the gun to her coat pocket and jammed

her fists to her hips as she faced him, all angry and fierce looking. "If you must know, I thought someone was following me and despite what you think, I did not want to have him catch up to me, so I rode hard. I circled back to see if he would follow my tracks, and he did. Then I led him on a wild chase. I must have outsmarted him, because I lost him."

"And in the process, you got lost too."

"I'd have found my way home if it hadn't started to snow. You can't blame me for that."

He considered her at length. So much like his pa and Esau. And maybe even a little bit like Pearl— taking risks with no concern for those who might be worried or worse…hurt by the consequences. Then, as if to prove him wrong on the last assessment, she moved to the window and rubbed a spot to peer through.

"Ma and Pa will be so worried."

He could not pretend he didn't hear the tightness in her voice. "They'll be relieved to learn you are safe and sound, not frozen stiff in the storm."

She grinned at him. "I guess that's one way of looking at it." Her amusement fled as she studied the interior of the house. "They aren't going to be pleased to learn where I'm being forced to stay."

"Forced." He barely stopped himself from stuttering. "I'm kind enough to offer you shelter."

Her blue eyes bored into him. "I think you know what I mean."

He couldn't deny it. "That's what comes of taking unnecessary risks." He kept repeating the words. They had become his protection and motto though he guessed they were wasted on his guest.

"You know Pa will insist you marry me." She looked thoughtful. "Of course, he doesn't have to know. I can return home and simply tell him I found shelter."

"I expect he'll want to know a bit more than that. Are you going to lie?"

"Maybe I just won't provide all the details. It wouldn't be lying to say I found a settler's shack and made myself at home."

He shook his head. "Things have a way of coming out."

"He won't learn all the facts from me. Are you going to tell him?"

"Me?" The last thing he wanted was to have a wife. Especially a wild rebel like this woman. "I don't want to get married."

"Especially to me, if I'm not mistaken."

Was he so obvious? "It's not personal."

She waved away his half apology. "At least we are agreed on that. I don't want to get married either."

He heard what she didn't say—especially to someone like him.

"He'll not learn from me where you've had to spend the night. But I won't lie." He glanced around the room. The reality of the situation slammed into him.

They were stuck here. They had to endure each other's company. Were they going to stay awake all night? How were they going to pass the hours together without his annoyance growing to the point he might consider sleeping in the cold of the barn?

CHAPTER 3

"We might as well bed down," Kade said.

Flora's mouth dried. Her tongue turned to wood. Bed down? How could she spend the night? She pressed to the window. "I never meant to cause Ma and Pa worry," she murmured to herself. A harmless ride. She'd done it many times, always making sure she returned home before her parents would grow concerned. Harmless fun, she'd said when Eve scolded her.

Thankfully, Kade didn't remind her that her choices had led to this situation.

"It wasn't my fault," she said as if he had given his opinion. "It was because of that man following me." Kade still said nothing.

But she heard his accusation as clearly as if he'd shouted it. Riding alone invited unwanted attention. Oh, wait. Those were Pa's words.

She pressed her forehead to the cold window and shivered. This was not going to turn out well unless she could make her parents believe she had spent the night alone.

Kade finally spoke. "You take the bed. I'll get my bedroll and sleep by the stove and keep the fire going."

She looked at the skiff of snow blowing in under the door. Her gaze followed Kade to the bedroom. It didn't even have a door. Just a wall between the kitchen cupboards and the cot.

He returned with a roll of bedding.

"You're going to sleep on the floor?"

"I've slept on far worse."

"Really? Like what?" She didn't truly care but delayed having to make a decision about how she would spend the night. Could she stand at the window and stare out? Could she go to the barn and sleep with the horses? It would be cold. Worse, she would be alone should that man appear. She shivered at the idea.

He plunked his bedding to the floor and sat on top of it.

She stared at the grin on his face. Goodness, he looked almost happy. Almost nice.

"I grew up accompanying my father and brother back and forth on the Santa Fe Trail. I learned to build a campfire, cook over it, and sleep on the ground by the time I was eight years old."

"The Santa Fe Trail." She sat on the nearest kitchen chair. "That is so exciting. Tell me all about it."

"Most days were monotonous. We hitched up and walked for the day. We stopped at noon for a quick meal. We stopped at dark for the evening meal. Even the food was monotonous. There were always chores to be done. It was hard work."

"But there must have been exciting parts. Did you see buffalo? Indians? Raging flood waters?"

"Yup. Saw hailstorms and lightning like you wouldn't think possible."

She leaned forward. "What was the most exciting thing you did or saw?"

He looked past her to the window. "One time I wandered away, looking for berries. Or maybe just looking for something to break the sameness." His gaze met hers, his eyes full of humor. "After all, I was only a kid." He continued to look at her as he spoke. "I found a den of fox kits. They were just old enough to be romping about. I sat and watched them for a while. They weren't afraid of me and soon played around my feet. They even let me touch them."

Flora stared at the way his memory wrapped his face in pleasure. Goodness, the man would be downright handsome if he learned to relax a bit. She released a longing sigh. "I would love to go on a wagon train journey."

"Where would you go?"

"Oregon. California. New Mexico. No, wait. I think I'd like to go north to the British Territories."

"There are rules there too. They have the North West Mounted Police and I hear they enforce their laws strictly."

She half scowled at him. "I am not a law breaker."

"Just a rule breaker?"

She huffed. "Who made all those dos and don'ts about how to live? Especially when there is no reason for them."

He studied her in hard silence.

She refused to blink before his stare. Just when her eyes began to water and she thought she couldn't hold his gaze any longer, he spoke.

"There is always a reason for a rule if a person cares to look for it."

Flora wanted to defend herself. Make him see that the things she did wouldn't hurt anyone. Not even herself. But her conscience stung. If she hadn't ridden so far, so fast, if she hadn't dressed like a man with no concern for her morals, she wouldn't be in this situation where her morals would surely be judged if she couldn't hide the truth. But more concerning to her was the knowledge that her parents would be beside themselves with worry.

She sprang to her feet and went to the window. Snow blew against the glass and built up on the outside ledge.

Another thud against the wall sent her heart into a frenzy. She turned to Kade. "You must have heard that."

"I hear the wind. Is that what you mean?"

"There might be something or someone out there."

He considered her with dark eyes and an accusing expression. "Perhaps your conscience is accusing you."

"Of what?"

"Maybe of being the cause of bringing danger to yourself and worry to your parents."

"Yeah, well, I never meant for this to happen. But I did hear something." She pulled the pistol from her coat pocket again and put it into her trousers pocket. "And I don't intend to sit here without being prepared." She ignored the way his eyebrows raised as if to point out that she might have thought of this sooner. Like before she left home. And certainly before she'd gone so far from town. "I know I should have headed for home as soon as I noticed that man tailing me."

"Why didn't you?"

She pushed her hair back from her face. "Horrible hair."

He laughed outright. "Certainly is unforgettable."

"It makes people stare at me. And feel free to touch it. Aren't there rules about touching people?"

"Suddenly you see the value of obeying rules?"

"I would never touch a stranger like that." She shuddered.

"Why didn't you turn back?"

"Guess it's too much to hope you'd let that go?"

"Yup."

She grinned at his lazy drawl. Then sobered as she admitted her reason. "I thought it would be a lark to outsmart the man."

"Proving you were more clever than he?"

"It was a mistake. I admit it." How had he managed to make her say that? Confessing a mistake was always so hard for her and yet here she was doing it when she didn't have to.

"I hope you learned something."

She grinned, thinking she could burst his bubble of satisfaction. "I learned lots. Like maybe I should have used my gun on him instead of running." She patted her pocket.

Kade laughed, but it sounded more mocking than amused. "Do you even know how to shoot that thing?"

"Of course I do. Pa showed me."

"How did you persuade him to do that?"

"Easy. I simply pointed out the fact that a rabid dog

might attack Ma out in the garden when Pa was away, and if no one knew how to shoot the gun to protect her…" She lifted her hands as if nothing more needed to be said.

"Your poor pa."

"It was the right thing to do." She hoped her voice sounded airy.

Kade laughed. "Of course it was."

She might have thought he was being critical but something in the way his eyes held hers made her wonder if he secretly admired her ability to get things done. A warm glow filled her heart to think someone might approve of her, even if secretly and momentarily.

"Flora, if you go to bed, I can get some sleep."

She jerked to her feet. "I'm sorry. I didn't mean to be keeping you up."

"Whoa. Settle down. I wasn't meaning any criticism. Only that morning will likely bring a break in the weather."

"I sure hope so." She scuttled to the bedroom. "Makes me think you don't appreciate my company," she murmured. Truth was, she had enjoyed learning more about Kade. She knew he would never have talked to her so frankly while surrounded by her sisters.

"Could work both ways."

She laid the pistol by the pillow and kicked off her boots. With a weary sigh she stretched out on the bed and pulled a quilt over herself. "Please, God," she murmured. "Bring an end to the storm and help Ma and Pa not to worry overmuch."

"You say something?" Kade called.

"Saying a prayer is all."

"I hope it was for safety."

"Shelter, safety, and adequate supplies." She quoted his short grace and was rewarded by his deep-throated chuckle.

"Good night, Miss Kinsley."

"Good night, Mr. Thomas." Another rumbling laugh.

Flora turned to her side and looked toward the other room. He had put out the lamp and total darkness surrounded her. But the little house was warm. She was safe. Tomorrow she would deal with the repercussions of being stranded overnight with a man she wasn't married to.

Nor did she wish to be married to him, especially given how much he disapproved of her.

* * *

KADE LAY ON THE FLOOR, wrapped in his bedroll. He had stuffed a blanket under the door to stop the draft, but the floor was still cold. However, the physical discomfort was nothing compared to the way his insides churned.

Preacher Kinsley would want to defend his daughter's virtue. Kade had to agree with Flora that it was best if the preacher didn't learn the exact details of her stay here.

He shifted about, seeking a comfortable position. Of all the people in the world, why did a red-haired rebel end up stranded in *his* house?

Something thudded against the side of the house. He'd heard the sound the previous two times. Likely a branch off a nearby tree.

He listened to make sure Flora didn't hear it and come flying out with her gun aimed at the door.

He didn't detect any shifting in the shadows and relaxed again. She must be asleep. He closed his eyes, knowing he'd likely lay awake all night. But sleep claimed him within a few minutes.

He couldn't say how much later it was that a sound jerked him from his slumbers.

He sat up and stared into the darkness, the skin on his arms twitching. What had he heard?

There it was again. Crying? Flora cried? He shook his head. Somehow he had expected she was too tough for that.

The sobs grew. Then she called out something.

His nerves jangled. Was there someone in there?

"Flora," he called. Then louder. "Flora, what's going on?"

The sobbing ended on a gasp.

"What's wrong?"

She cleared her throat. "Nothing."

"I heard you cry out. Sounds like you were calling someone. Is there someone in there?"

She made a dismissive sound. "You mean you would sleep through an intruder entering your house and coming to this room? That's not very reassuring."

"No, of course I wouldn't. But who were you calling?"

"It was a dream. I have them often. It means nothing."

"Oh." He got up and put more wood on the fire. "What were you dreaming about? Or who?"

"I don't know. I never remember what my dream is about."

He settled down again, but the sound of her cries echoed in his head. "You seemed distressed."

"Eve says the same. But I honestly don't know what I was dreaming."

"Don't you find it unsettling?"

She didn't answer immediately, and he wondered if she was crying silently. "Kade, it doesn't bother me, because I don't remember. What bothers me is you not letting me go back to sleep."

A burst of laughter broke from his throat at her dry tone. "Yes, ma'am. I'll be quiet now." Except he kept chortling to himself.

Flora called, "Sure doesn't sound quiet to me."

Her words served only to increase his amusement and he laughed loud and long. He sobered enough to hear a long-suffering sigh and turned his face to his pillow to muffle his chuckles.

He woke the next morning to a cold house and hurried to start the fire.

Flora stepped from the room, her hair swept back into an untidy braid that she'd secured with a strip of rag. Did she carry bits with her for this purpose? He didn't realize he stared at the thick braid until she touched it.

"It's the best I could do under the circumstances."

"Sorry. I was only wondering where you got the tie."

Her eyes flashed that dark blue he'd noticed before. "Could be I tore it off the edge of your sheet."

"You didn't. You wouldn't." He sputtered his words.

She tipped her head back and laughed, a merry sound that made him think the sun had broken through. But a glance at the window showed it to be frost covered.

"Didn't say I did. Just said I could have." She chuckled as he stared at her. "It's off the hem of my shirt."

With a bemused shake of his head, he went to the

window and scraped a peephole. "It's still storming. Can't see as far as the corner of the house."

"It's early yet. Surely it will stop snowing when the sun comes up."

"True. In the meantime, how does coffee sound?"

"Kaw-fee."

"What?"

Her wide-eyed innocent look almost fooled him until he realized she had answered his question literally. Her dead-pan humor was so unexpected that he blinked once, twice, and then laughed. "I think it will taste better than it sounds."

"Good. What's for breakfast? I could cook something. What do you have besides potatoes and eggs?"

"That was the last of my eggs until I get to town again. I really should get some hens, but who would look after them when I'm out on the range?"

She opened the cupboard doors. "You said you had adequate supplies."

He reached past her to indicate what he had. "Beans, flour, cornmeal…" He listed all his supplies. "The basics."

"Seems you're into basics both in prayers and supplies." She turned and came face to face with him, his arm still stretched over her shoulder.

He couldn't be sure but guessed it was shock that widened her eyes. Shock and surprise at discovering him so close. He had only to lower his arms to embrace her. Which he was not going to do. Ever.

He quickly stepped away and tried to remember what they had been talking about. Yes, the basics.

"It's all I need."

She turned back to the cupboards. "I'll make some griddle cakes if you have syrup or jam to go on them."

"I have syrup." He retrieved the tin from the far cupboard, away from Flora and the awkwardness between them. He set it on the table as she mixed up batter. She eyed the frying pan with its layer of bacon fat then shrugged and dropped batter into the hot fat.

"How long you been here?" she asked.

He gladly turned to normalcy. "About a year."

"You a homesteader?" She began to pile pancakes on a plate.

"Nope. A rancher. I have a small herd."

"Oh yes, I remember you mentioned that you and your brother wanted to ranch together."

"I made it. He didn't." He kept his tone as flat as the pancakes piling up on the plate. He'd learned to ignore the pain that shafted through him at every remembrance of Esau.

"I expect you miss him still."

"Every day."

"Where are your cows during this storm?"

"I hope they've found shelter in the trees south of here."

She gave him a considering look. "Seems to me ranching is risky business."

He wondered momentarily at the way she studied him. "It can be."

She flipped three more pancakes.

His mouth began to water.

"You sure it's wise to take such a risk?"

"It's worth it." He kept his eyes on the plate of

35

pancakes as she carried it to the table and sat down across from him.

"So you'd agree that some risks are worth taking?"

"I'd agree with that."

"Well, then, it seems we are finally agreed. Are you going to say grace?" She bowed her head.

"Agreed on what?"

"Say grace," she murmured.

"I can't."

Her head came up. "Why not?"

"Because I have an unanswered question consuming my thoughts."

She shrugged. "Seems a man of your convictions should be able to control such things." Her eyes were darkest blue, almost emotionless, and yet he wasn't convinced that she wasn't turning his words into something they didn't mean.

He sucked in air and bowed his head. "Thanks for the food and a warm house. Amen."

"Amen," she echoed and speared herself four pancakes, dowsing them in syrup.

He followed her example but paused before he lifted a mouthful. "I'm sure we agree on many things, but what were you meaning?"

She waved her fork, indicating he should wait until she'd swallowed. "Seems obvious to me. We agree that some risks are worth taking."

He enjoyed a mouthful of breakfast as he mulled over his answer. "Trouble is, I don't think we mean the same thing. I was talking about ranching, where a man faces challenges in the hopes of building up something solid."

"But a storm, disease, animals, even rustlers, could

leave you with nothing. You could be hurt. Get sick. Lose everything in a fire."

"Aren't you the perfect pessimist?"

She shrugged. "Don't you see? You can live in fear of what might be, or you can embrace life and enjoy it. I think God meant for us to do the latter." She said it with a finality that indicated the conversation was over in her mind.

"Without regard for the consequences, I suppose?"

She faced him squarely. "No, I think a person should consider the risks involved, but that shouldn't be the only factor in a decision."

He shook his head. "I doubt you and I will ever agree on this subject, but I will be interested in seeing how you like the consequence of your choice to ride so far from town yesterday."

She glanced at the window. The outdoors was a foggy white indicating the sun had risen. "It's still storming." She sighed.

They finished eating and carried their dishes to the cupboard to wash up.

Once they finished, Flora went to the window. "What is Pa going to say?"

"I can guess. I'm sure you can too." If this storm lasted all day and into another night... Well, the preacher was going to demand more of an explanation than Flora had prepared.

"No." She rocked her head back and forth. "He can't make us marry. We don't even like each other. You think I'm irresponsible and I think..."

"What?" How did she view him?

"I think you're afraid to live life to the full."

CHAPTER 4

Flora remained at the window. She wouldn't admit it aloud, but this was one occasion when she wished she hadn't been so rash...had been content to ride close to town. She should have listened to the warnings inside her head. And true to Pa's predictions, she was going to reap the consequences.

The storm showed no sign of letting up no matter how hard she stared at it nor how hard she begged God to bring it to an end.

Her foot went to sleep from standing in one position too long and she turned from the window with a weary sigh.

It'd been some time since Kade had spoken. In fact, it seemed he hadn't said anything since her pronouncement that he was afraid to live. Her gaze went to his macabre collection of reminders of his losses.

"Why do you want to remember that?" She pointed toward the items.

"There are some things I can't forget."

"I suppose that's true. Just like there are some things I can't remember." At his questioning look, she explained. "Like my dream. Why can't I remember something that seems to bother me so much when I'm asleep?"

He had turned to look at the things on the bookshelf. Lines grooved his face as if recalling the pain of his losses.

"I'm sorry for saying you're afraid to live."

His gaze shifted toward her. "Did you mean it?"

"I—" Part of her did, but she couldn't say that. "I don't know you well enough to know if I do or not." There were things she wanted to ask him. "Will it bother you to talk about them?" She tipped her head toward the bookshelf.

"I don't know. Can't say as I ever have."

She sat down. Waved him toward the chair opposite.

He refilled their coffee cups and sat.

"Tell me about your father."

"What do you want to know?"

"Was he on the Santa Fe trail when he died? What did he do? Where was your mother?"

"We were on the trail." He began slowly. "We'd run into a deep draw that was going to be a challenge to cross. We'd crossed down a ways on previous trips, but a spring flood had washed that deeper so this was the best place unless the scout found us something better. We were waiting for the scout to return. Pa said he wasn't going to wait while everyone jawed about what to do. He said he'd crossed steep draws before." As Kade spoke, his volume and speed increased.

"He drove the wagon to the edge of the cliff. I knew

from the beginning that he was doing something foolish. The other freighters said it was too risky. He'd lose everything trying to take his wagon down that slope. They said wait until the scout found a safer place, but Pa said some things are worth the risk. He cut thick branches and put them between the spokes of the wheels, chaining them up tight. He hung heavy trees on the back of the wagon to slow its descent." Kade swallowed hard. "I remember how I was so afraid I thought I would throw up as I watched Pa walking beside the oxen and driving them forward."

He paused. His gaze had grown distant.

Flora knew he was seeing the past just as she was picturing every detail as he talked and feeling every emotion...the fear of seeing his pa go stubbornly ahead. The dust from the trailing trees. The crash and rattle of the wagons.

He continued. "At first I thought it would be okay. The men around me seemed to think so too. They slapped each other's backs." Kade's voice deepened. "And then it happened."

He stopped. His face had grown pale. His mouth tight. His eyes filled with black despair. "One back wheel hit a bump and lifted off the ground. The oxen bolted. It all happened so fast and yet the moment seemed to last forever. Pa ordering the oxen to stop. The wagon slowly lifting off the ground and sailing forward. And dropping in an explosion of goods, wood, wheels, and canvas."

Kade spoke slowly as if each word he spoke hurt his throat. "I tried to see my pa. The men skidded down the slope, sliding and clutching at bushes to slow their descent. Esau scrambled down to join the men. I wanted to go too but hands held me back. I could only watch as they tossed aside crates and shattered wood. There was Pa. They carried him up the hill and lay him on the ground. Someone pushed me forward.

"I remember how my feet refused to move and my tongue wouldn't work.

"The men stood around with their hats in their hand. And I knew. I just knew. It was Esau who pulled me to my feet. 'It's over,' he said.

"He didn't have to do it," I yelled. "He could have waited."

Several said he only did what he thought he could do. He didn't expect to fail.

"He could have waited." I think I said it a hundred times over the next few days. I was a twelve-year-old orphan with only an older brother to take care of me. And him only sixteen. Esau assured me we would be okay on our own. After all, he had been doing a man's work for a long time."

Silence hung like a pall over the room as he ended his story.

Flora's heart filled with tears. A young boy alone on the trail. "Somehow being on the Santa Fe Trail doesn't sound quite so appealing anymore."

"That was our last trip."

"Then what did you do?"

"We drove cattle from Texas north. I saw Montana Territory on our second drive. That's when Esau and I decided we would start a ranch here."

She knew what had happened to Esau. She knew his ma had died when he was eight. He'd said something about a girl he planned to marry who had run off with someone else. What a horrible life he'd had.

Made it easy to understand why he had such a guarded view of life. But his life had to have been more than pain and tragedy. "What's a good memory you have?"

He tipped back in his chair and studied the ceiling then lowered his chair to all fours. "I don't remember a lot about my ma. Nor can I explain why Pa took us on the trail with him from the time we were young. Every time we returned to Santa Fe we stayed with Ma. We got new clothes too. My happiest memory is silly. I hardly remember Ma, but the one thing I remember is the days we were with her in Santa Fe. I remember the warmth of the house, the comfort of the beds."

He gave her a lopsided grin. "A person can get tired of sleeping on the ground, being cold or hot or wet and uncomfortable at best." He shifted his gaze past her. "I recall having her tuck the covers around me at night and sitting at a table with her every morning having tea for breakfast. Tea made in a china pot—it was a very special teapot. Ma said Pa had given it to her on their wedding day. It was squat and white and had red roses on it. She served our tea in china cups with saucers. I knew that kings and queens must have tea served in china just like that. And she always made a chocolate cake for us. Isn't it strange that I remember all that but I can't picture my ma at all?"

Flora smiled, her heart soothed by this sweet story. "But you just have—you've seen her heart with your heart."

* * *

HE STARED at her like he'd never seen her before. This wild rebel of a gal had unexpected depths to her. An insight into life that he'd not seen or experienced elsewhere.

Maybe he could offer her something as well. Though if her father learned that she had spent the night here, Kade would be offering to marry her, whether he wanted to or not.

It wasn't something he cared to think about at the moment.

"Tell me about your family."

She shrugged one shoulder. "What's to know? You've met most of us. You've heard Pa preach and you've eaten at our table."

"I didn't see anyone very clearly at that time."

Her eyes narrowed. "Seems to me you saw enough to pass judgment on me."

He would not go down that trail again. It led nowhere. "Were the others adopted as babies?"

Her eyebrows quirked as if she recognized his desire to avoid the other conversation. She smiled and nodded, silently agreeing. "Adele and Tilly were adopted as babies. Josie was twelve when she came, and we think Victoria was about fifteen."

"You think? Why don't you know?"

Flora grinned as if enjoying his surprise and confusion. "She'd been in an accident and completely lost her memory. No one knew who she was or where she'd come from. Ma and Pa took her in and named her Victoria because they said she would overcome her injuries and the loss of her memory."

"Wow. I'm trying to imagine what it would be like to have everything in your life wiped out when you're mostly grown." He shifted his gaze to the mementos on his bookshelf.

"Might be easier." Flora's voice was soft.

"Maybe. But I would forget the good as well as the bad. I don't think I'd like that."

"She's very accepting of it. She's such a sweet person."

Kade returned his attention to Flora. "Coming from you, I would think that is high praise."

Her eyes narrowed. "What do you mean?"

He held her gaze unblinkingly. "I don't think you give your approval very readily."

Their look went on and on. He determined he would not be the first one to pull away.

Finally, she sighed. "Too many people judge, rather than accept. Victoria doesn't. She says she has no idea who or what she was in the past so has no right to judge others. I like that."

She hadn't said anything about him but Kade felt condemned, nevertheless. He'd been quick to judge Flora rather than try and understand her. He was beginning to see how her past had shaped the way she lived, just as his had shaped him. And who was to say either of them was entirely correct? Like she said, he was afraid to live freely. And she, perhaps, lived a bit too freely. Perhaps they were both right to a degree and wrong as well.

"I have a brother—" She broke off. Her mouth opened and closed. She blinked rapidly.

Concerned that she seemed confused, he leaned

forward and touched the back of her hand. "Flora, what's wrong?"

She jerked, swallowed loudly. "I don't know. Anyway, Josh is a brother to all of us. He's the oldest. The only one who isn't adopted."

Kade sat back. "I haven't met him."

"He's not with us."

"You mean—?"

She chuckled. "He's not dead, if that's what you're thinking. Or at least, we hope he isn't. But he is missing. We haven't had any word from him in almost two years. It's one of the reasons Ma and Pa moved out here. He'd headed for Montana Territory, and they hope they'll be able to locate him. I surely do miss him." Her gaze went beyond him into the distance, perhaps seeing things in the past.

"Tell me about him." Kade spoke softly, knowing Flora was dealing with emotions concerning the absence of her brother.

She began, her voice low and soft as she remembered. "Josh is eight years older than me. So, when I arrived in the family, he was twelve. I idolized him. He treated me like an equal rather than the annoying little sister I likely was. I followed him everywhere. He taught me how to throw a ball, swing a rope, and tie knots. But by the time I was seven he didn't like me following him when he met up with his friends. I did it anyway, sneaking about and not letting them see me. I recall one time..." She chuckled. "Josh's friend found me spying on them. He caught me and yanked my braids." She rubbed her head as if remembering the pain of having her hair pulled so hard. "Then he called me a sneaky redhead. It made me so angry. I ran into the woods. I got busy playing and forgot the time until I realized how dark it had become. Ma would be upset with me for running off. I hurried home only to discover that she had visitors and hadn't even noticed I was gone. That kind of hurt. I expected she would worry about me. Later Josh told me he was sorry, but he didn't want to be looking out for his baby sister when he was hanging around with his friends. Baby sister. I was so angry, but I didn't argue with him. I just walked away. 'Cause I had learned something that day. I could have my freedom if I made sure Ma didn't know about it." The words had come out in a breathless rush.

Kade smiled in spite of himself. "Seems that's how you live your life."

She brought her gaze to him. "What do you mean?"

"Do what you want so long as your parents don't find out about it."

"You make me sound like a rebellious child."

Rebellious, yes. Child, no. But Kade kept his thoughts to himself.

"I'm not." She looked at the window. "One of the things Pa says often is, 'Be sure your sins will find you out.' He usually adds, 'Let not your good be evil spoken of.' Seems I'm going to pay for my afternoon of freedom."

She would not be the only one who paid the price for her choice, but he had no desire to deal with what the future threatened at the moment.

"What is a good memory of yours?" he asked.

She met his gaze and held it.

He could tell she was searching for an answer to his question. "I'm surprised you take so long to answer. I thought your family seemed happy."

"We are. And there are lots of really fun things to tell you about. Like when Adele had her baby." Flora sighed. "I almost cried to hold that perfect little boy. So tiny and yet everything complete." The blue of her eyes flashed like a rushing stream as she described her nephew.

Kade couldn't take his eyes off her as she told about holding the newborn and examining his hands and feet. He would never have thought her to be the sort to be so touched by a new life. He seemed to be finding more and more surprising, unexpected facets to this woman.

She grinned at him. "I'm gushing, aren't I?"

He chuckled. "I've heard babies do strange and wonderful things to women."

"Pshaw. Women? You should have seen Pa. He couldn't take his eyes off the little guy and insisted he was the best possible person to comfort him when he cried."

She leaned back. "Of course, there are lots of happy fun times in our family."

"Then why do you sound regretful?"

"I don't know. Sometimes I feel like there's something missing."

"Like what?"

"I don't know. I wish I did."

"Is that why you ride like you do? Maybe why you do some of the other things you do? Are you looking for something?"

She chuckled but it sounded more mocking than amused. "I don't know."

He wanted to remove the hollowness in her eyes. "So, if you could pick just one memory to keep, what would it be?"

She rocked her head back and forth. "I think I am still waiting for it to happen." She sprang to her feet and circled the room, trailing her fingers along the top shelf of the bookcase, staring a moment at Esau's reins. She shook her head and moved on. She touched the top of the trunk in the corner and came to a halt in front of the window.

Her restlessness made him want to catch her, hold her, and calm her down. "What would you be doing on such a day if you were at home?"

She spun about to face him, her face alight with amusement. "Ma would have us busy. There's always mending to do, socks and mittens to knit. Bread and cookies to bake. Dusting. And if our work was done, we could read, or play games."

"Games? Like what?"

"Checkers."

There was no missing the note of glee in her answer.

She continued. "I'm a pretty fair hand at the game if I do say so myself. And we have several jigsaw puzzles. Ma and Eve really like them." She added the latter with far less enthusiasm.

"Checkers. Well, why didn't you say so?" He went to the bookshelf and found the board and the game pieces. He was good at the game too, though he'd let her discover that herself.

She rubbed her hands and chortled as he set the game out on the table. "Prepare to be soundly whooped."

They bent over the game, concentrating and considering each possible option. He felt her intensity, saw it in the flash in her eyes after every move. He felt they were evenly matched, countering each other's moves. But she was good.

With a shout of victory, she took his last checker.

"I won. I won. I told you I was good."

"Bet your pa also told you not to gloat. There's nothing worse than a bragging winner."

"Except a sore loser." She gave a playful punch to his shoulder and laughed.

"Ow." He grabbed his arm and pretended pain.

"That was just a tap." She threatened to repeat the action.

He caught her fist and held it in the air between them.

Her gaze met his, fractured with humor, teasing and something more. Something that made his mouth grow dry. He dropped her hand. "Don't hit."

"Another game?" She arranged the checkers without waiting for him to reply.

"This time I'll try to win."

She chuckled. "You'll have to try awfully hard."

She won three games in a row, but during the last game he realized something. She had the same plan each time. It was a good one. He played the moves through in his mind until he saw where he could outmaneuver her. In the fourth game he let her do as she'd previously done then he made an unexpected move.

She stared at him. "What are you doing?"

"Winning."

"No way." She studied the board long and hard then moved.

He counter-moved.

She studied the board for some time, then said, "I'm getting hungry."

He glanced at the clock. How did it get to be almost twelve? He looked out the window. "It's still storming."

She pushed aside the game and stood.

"I should have been planning something to eat instead of wasting my time on a game," she grumbled.

"Nothing worse than a sore loser," he reminded her.

"I haven't lost yet. Let's make soup." She peeled carrots as he peeled potatoes. They threw it all into a pot of water, adding chopped onions and salt and pepper. She looked through the cupboards for more ingredients.

She found a can of tomatoes and handed it to him to open.

He dumped it in as she tossed in a few spices.

He tasted the mixture. "Not bad." He offered her a spoonful and she leaned closer to sip the sample.

"It's pretty good." Her gaze met his, and the air sizzled with something he couldn't identify.

He jerked away to cover the pot.

As they waited for the soup to cook, he took down two large soup bowls.

She carried spoons to the table, lingering to study the checkerboard.

Kade chuckled. "'Fraid you'll lose?"

She shook a spoon at him. "The game isn't over until it's over."

He grabbed the spoon and shook it at her. "Which it soon will be."

Flora reached for the spoon, but just before she clasped it, he jerked it away.

She gave a snort of laughter and again reached for it. He held it just out of reach.

Her laughter welled up like a bubbling fountain and

then it choked off and she dropped her hands to her side. Her face seemed to fold in on itself. Her lips quivered. Her eyes filled with tears.

"Flora, what's wrong?"

She didn't seem to hear him.

He caught her by the shoulders and gave her a little shake. "What's going on?"

CHAPTER 5

"*F*lora. Talk to me."

Kade's strident voice reached Flora's brain. She blinked and stared into his concerned eyes.

"What happened?" he asked.

"I don't know. I felt like I had done that before."

"Done what?" His hands rested on her shoulders, anchoring her in the present.

"Tried to catch a spoon." She sought words to explain. "It was like I was somewhere else. With someone else. I think I was remembering something, but I can't remember what." She sucked in air. "I'm sorry. It doesn't make any more sense to me than it does to you."

They studied each other as if hoping to find an explanation, but none came to her and obviously none came to him. He must think her strange as well as wild.

She shook her head and stepped toward the stove. As soon as Kade's arms dropped from her shoulders, she wished she hadn't moved. Her insides jittered with uncertainty. His hands had steadied her.

She stirred the soup and tasted it. "It's done." He held out the bowls as she ladled soup into them and then he carried them to the table.

They sat down and she bowed her head as he prayed. At his, "amen," she lifted her head to look at him.

"If it is a memory, why don't I remember?"

"I don't know. I wish I could help you."

They bent over their bowls. The only sounds were of the clock ticking, the wind, snow against the house, and the spoons clinking against the china of the bowls.

Flora paused to look at the spoon in her hand. She'd held spoons plenty of times and not had this flash of a past memory. Why now? And what did it mean? She searched her brain, looking for an answer, and found none. With a deep sigh, she pushed aside her empty bowl and glanced at the window.

"Will this storm ever end?" She knew she sounded petulant, but she couldn't help it. The longer she was stranded here, the less likely she could bluff her way out of the facts.

Kade chuckled. "Spring has always come. It always will. Winter just likes to think it's always the winner even though it isn't." His gaze went to the checker game and Flora laughed.

It was good to think of something besides what would happen when she returned to town. And even what memory she failed to remember.

She gathered up the used dishes. "First, we clean up."

He stood and saluted sharply. "Yes, ma'am."

For half a second, she wondered if he'd been offended by the way she ordered him around, but he grinned widely and his eyes brimmed with amusement.

"Sorry, I guess I sound like my ma. Didn't mean to."

He followed her to the cupboard and took a bowl to dry as she washed it. "I can think of worse things." He nudged her shoulder. "Sounding like a freighter, for instance." He shook his head. "Some of them are very crude. I remember hearing some colorful words when I was on my first trip with Pa. I thought they sounded different, so I used them. Pa said if he ever heard such language from my mouth again, he would skin me alive."

"Did he?"

"What? Skin me alive?" He gave his arms and legs serious study. "I don't think so." He tried to sound confused, but she knew he teased.

She laughed. "Did he hear that kind of language from you again?"

"Nope. I knew better than to test my pa." He put away the bowls and spoons then rubbed his hands. "You ready to finish that game?"

"Are you ready to be defeated?" They returned to the table.

She studied the board, trying to understand his plan. Then she made her move.

He made his immediately, as if he knew what she was going to do. She saw that he could win but she kept playing, hoping he would make a mistake.

He captured her last king and leaned back. "I won."

"Yes, you did, but considering how great a victory this is, shouldn't you smile or cheer?"

His face remained impassive. "I'm cheering on the inside, but I refuse to be a gloating winner."

"You're missing out. Gloating is half the fun of winning." She squinted at him. "Oh, come on." She got to her feet and held out her hands to him. "I'll show you how it's done."

He hesitated, looking as if he suspected her of having a trick up her sleeve, then slowly got to his feet.

She grabbed his hands and lifted them up in a victory salute. "Now you say, 'I won. I won.' And you pump your fist like this." She left his hands in midair and showed him what she meant.

He stared at her.

She planted her hands on her hips. "You're not taking this seriously."

"I'm supposed to?"

"Yes, you are. Now give it a little effort."

He pumped one fist in the air. "Like this?"

"And say—"

"I won. I won."

She patted his shoulder. "You got it."

They both collapsed into laughter. Their amusement ended and she stared into his dark brown eyes. Strange how she'd never noticed before how much they revealed about him. His conscientiousness, his humor, his—

She jerked away. "Do you want another game?"

He looked out the window. "It shows no sign of letting up. I better get more water and wood and take care of the horses." He pulled on his heavy coat, a hat with ear flaps, and leather mitts with knitted liners, then grabbed the buckets. "I'll be back shortly."

She stepped between him and the door. "It's thick as pea soup. What if you get lost or turned around?"

He squeezed her shoulder. "Flora, I made sure when I planned my place that everything was laid out so I could find it in the dark or in a storm." She didn't move.

"I'll be okay. You stay by the door and open it when you hear me. My hands will be full." He lifted the empty buckets as if to prove it to her.

She nodded and reluctantly stepped aside to hold the door open. Snow swirled into the house and the warmth sucked from the room. She couldn't see more than a foot from where she stood. As soon as he was out, she closed the door and shivered.

She remained at the door, counting the seconds. The clock grew louder with each tick. Her heart struggled to beat as the moments passed. Shouldn't he be back by now? What if he got lost? She'd go in search of him but then wouldn't they both end up lost?

Her thoughts went 'round and 'round, anticipating and trying to resolve every possibility.

Something thudded at the door and she jerked it open. He stood before her crusted with snow. She stepped aside and he hurried in. He put the buckets of water on the cupboard then held his mittened hands over the stove.

"It's fierce out there. The wind has a nasty bite to it."

She wished he didn't have to go out again, but she eyed the woodbox and knew there wasn't enough to see them through the day.

"What if the storm lasts overnight again?" Her brain felt hollow at the thought.

"We're safe and warm. That's all that matters for now."

For now. She wasn't one to dwell on what might happen later, but there would be hard questions to answer when she got home.

He headed for the door and she waited to let him in when he returned with his arms full of wood.

Again, the minutes ticked by accompanied by the loud clock. Time stretched into eternity and back but still, he didn't bang at the door.

If something happened to him, she'd be alone. The edges of the room sucked in on her.

A thud against the door jerked her from her fears and she yanked it open.

"Thank goodne—" The words died on her tongue as she stared into the face of a stranger. The man who had been trailing her.

He jerked the door from her hand and slammed it shut then smirked at her. "Knew I'd catch up to yous sooner or later. No one can get away from Eagle Pete."

* * *

KADE CARRIED AS much wood as his arms would hold, making it next to impossible for him to reach for the doorknob. He struggled against the wind, concentrating on how many steps he would need to reach the corner of the house. Ten. He stuck his foot out to feel for the wall. Nothing. He closed his eyes and considered the problem. No doubt his steps were shorter because of the wind he fought and the load he carried. He took one more step and then another. And ran into the house. His breath released in a cold rush. He eased forward, making sure to keep the wall to his left. He knew when he reached the door and banged his foot against it. It would be a relief to be out of the wind and into the warmth of the house.

Was kind of nice to think of having company as he sat out the storm.

Had he not banged hard enough? He kicked at the door again and waited. The snow seeped under his collar and the cold made his bones hurt.

Seems Flora had gotten distracted and forgotten to wait to open the door for him.

Wasn't that just like her? Only thinking of herself.

He fumbled trying to reach the door handle without losing his load and burst into the room. His insides froze at what he saw, and he immediately regretted his harsh and undeserved judgment of her.

Flora stood on one side of the table, her eyes never leaving the man who dodged one direction and then the other as he tried to reach her. She darted from side to side, avoiding him.

"What's going on?" Kade demanded, his tone low and firm. The same way he would speak to uncooperative oxen.

The man stood still. "I don't need no interference."

"Looks to me like the lady doesn't want your attention." Kade didn't change his tone or his volume.

"Sure she does. She just don't know it yet." The man's laugh was mocking and evil sounding. "I 'tend to change her mind." He lunged for her.

Flora avoided him and dashed toward Kade to stand beside him, pressing to his load of wood.

Her breathing was too rapid. Likely her heartbeat was too.

The man faced them, allowing Kade to get a good look at him. He was built like a slab of granite. His face held gouges as if carved from the same hunk of rock by a man with a dull knife and little care for the results. His black bushy eyebrows shaded equally black eyes that showed a gleam of madness. He was unshaven, his skin darkened by years of going unwashed.

Kade decided to try the direct route though he had little faith it would work. "This is my house. You aren't welcome here. Please leave."

"Not until I get what I came for." He leered at Flora.

The muscles in Kade's neck tightened. Nothing Flora had done made it okay for a man to look at her like that. "I'm asking you nicely to leave." His voice grew firmer even as his insides coiled into a tight spring.

"Ask all ya want." The man didn't so much as shift his gaze to Kade. "But ya can't make me."

"That's where you're wrong." Kade took two steps forward, forcing the man to look at him.

"Get out of my way." A big arm came out to push Kade aside.

Kade dropped his load of wood. The pieces rolled down the man's shins and landed on his feet.

The intruder jerked, reaching to rub his feet. "That done hurt." He straightened, his face twisted with anger.

But Kade had already jumped out of his reach, intending to reach his rifle from beside the stove.

"Stop right there," Flora said, her voice as hard as the ice on the water trough. "Or I'll shoot."

The man stared at the gun she gripped in both her hands. Kade noted with satisfaction that she had cocked it.

The man laughed. "I ain't scared of no woman." He stepped toward her, but the hunks of wood were in his way. He kicked at them.

Kade had reached his rifle and jabbed it in the man's back. The man's hands went up as if he thought he could persuade Kade that he meant no harm.

"Be afraid," Kade said. "Be very afraid. Now make your way to the door before she shoots you. I assure you, she can, and she will."

"It's snowing out." A whine in the man's voice made Kade want to shoot him on the spot. "You gonna make me go out there in a storm?"

"You came from the storm."

"I had something to do." He leered again at Flora then thought better of it with two firearms threatening him. "I'll freeze."

"Let the wind take you south. Stay close to the trees and you should find an old abandoned shack out there." He nudged the man toward the door and outside. Kade stayed on his heels. The man had tied his horse to the corral fence. The poor animal was so covered in snow it was impossible to tell its color. Kade waited for him to take his horse then followed him until he was certain he wouldn't shelter in one of the outbuildings.

He hurried back to the house and eased the door open. "It's me. Don't shoot."

Flora lowered her gun. Kade closed the door and went to her side.

She shook. He kicked aside the wood and led her to a chair, eased her to the seat, and squatted in front of her.

"Are you okay?" He tossed off his mittens and squeezed her hands.

She looked deep into his eyes, as if searching for something. He let her look, let her see that he cared that such a man had threatened her.

She swallowed loudly. "Do you think he'll come back?"

"I'll bar the door. He won't get in."

She nodded. "It's the same man who followed me."

"I guessed it was." He rubbed his thumbs across the back of her hands.

Her limbs stopped shaking and she gave a nervous-sounding laugh. "I guess I brought this on myself."

He stood and pulled her to her feet. "You are not responsible for the actions of a man like that, no matter what you do."

She tipped her head and looked into his eyes. A tiny smile creased her eyes and teased at her mouth. "Is this the same man who accused me of being foolish? Wasn't that just a day ago? My, how your opinion has changed."

It was true. She might be a rebel in many ways, but she wasn't foolhardy, as he'd once thought. "Don't get too smug." He tweaked her nose. And couldn't break free of her gaze. It was like being sucked into warm water, finding comfort on a cold day.

She grinned. "I'll try not to."

It took him a moment to realize she referred to his warning to not get smug.

She looked at the wood scattered across the floor. "Good weapon you had there." She began to pick up the pieces and stack them beside the stove.

He gathered up wood as well. But when he turned to carry it to the stove, he bumped into her. Her eyes flashed with surprise and maybe something more. Was it awareness? Perhaps admiration? "Thanks for rescuing me," she said.

"You're welcome. Glad I was able to." So it was gratitude. What did he expect?

And why did it matter? She was here under his care and protection. Nothing more. And if her father caught even a whiff of his changing feelings, there would be a wedding in his near future.

Wedded to a rebel was not in his plans.

CHAPTER 6

*a*s Flora helped stack the wood neatly she told herself over and over that her shaky nerves were from dealing with the intruder. Not from a shift in her feelings toward Kade. He had rescued her. Of course, she was filled with gratitude. It was nothing more than that.

She grabbed the broom and swept the chips from the floor.

Done with that, she circled the room several times, ignoring Kade's curiosity as he leaned against the kitchen cupboard watching her.

"Another game of checkers?" he asked.

She shook her head and stared out the window.

"It's not letting up."

He said nothing. There was no need. They both knew it was getting too late in the afternoon to make it to town even if the storm stopped in the next half hour.

"Another night here." She hoped she sounded calm.

"Is it so bad?"

She faced him, trying to read his expression, but he revealed nothing. She shrugged. "It's better than a lot of things I can think of."

"Yeah?"

"Yeah. Like being out in the cold. Like sharing the place with"—she shuddered—"the likes of him." She glanced toward the door. "I'll be looking over my shoulder for a long time."

"And staying close to home, I hope."

"So, it comes back to that. I can't say as I'm surprised." She went to the bookshelf and stared at the objects on it.

"Flora, please promise me you won't take any risks with that man out there somewhere. I suspect he's not the sort to give up easily."

She brought her gaze to his but instead of seeing judgment, she thought she saw concern. It left her unable to think.

"Promise?" he insisted.

She shook her head. "I'm not stupid enough to do something that gives him a chance to get near me." But she couldn't bring herself to give a promise. It carried too much weight. Too much expectation. As if he would check on her to make sure she kept her promise, although she didn't expect to see him again once she returned home...unless she saw him at church.

Unless, heaven forbid, they were forced to marry.

The storm continued. They had several hours to while away before nightfall. Her insides felt cramped and crowded. Ma would say work would cure that.

"Let's make something." She went to the kitchen.

He straightened and edged away from the cupboard. "Like what? Chocolate cake?"

At the anticipation in his voice, she decided that was the ideal activity. "Sure, though it might not be like what your mother made." She checked the temperature on the oven. "About right." Then pulled out a bowl.

"What can I do?"

"You want to help?" She'd thought he'd stand around watching.

"Can't I?"

"I don't see any reason you can't."

"I might learn how to make it for myself."

"There's an idea." She grinned at him. "Why don't I tell you what to do and this can be your first cake.

It will be, won't it?"

He seemed suddenly interested in opening the cupboards and looking at the contents.

She poked her head under his elbow to look in his face.

He avoided her eyes.

"You know how to bake a cake?"

He ducked behind a cupboard door. "I did try once."

Flora pulled him around so she could look at him. "Yes?"

He grinned. "It was a total flop. I had to throw it out. Even the coyotes and crows wouldn't touch it."

She burst out laughing. When she could speak, she patted his shoulder. "Let's see if you can't do better this time." Step by step, she gave him directions, from greasing the pan to measuring the ingredients. Thankfully, Ma had taught her daughters how to make a decent cake without eggs.

He beat the batter, spread it in the pan, and gingerly

placed it in the oven. He handed her a spoon. "Want to help me lick out the bowl?"

Their heads almost touched as they scraped the remnants of the batter from the bowl.

"It tastes good," he said.

"It will taste even better when you take it out of the oven."

The bowl was licked so clean it almost didn't have to be washed.

"Can you write the recipe down for me?" He brought her a piece of paper and a pencil.

She wrote it down, complete with step-by-step instructions.

"Ma always iced the cake," he said, hope clinging to his words.

"So should you then."

"Me?"

"Of course. You want to be able to do this on your own, don't you?"

"Yes, but I thought I was pushing my luck by trying to make a cake."

"Trying? Ho. I think you did it. You just have to wait for it to bake." He reached for the oven handle. "And no peeking yet."

Again, she talked him through the process of making fudge frosting. He beat it to creaminess and tasted it. He closed his eyes and sighed. "I do believe that's even better than Ma made."

"And you did it yourself. While we wait for the cake to bake, what's for supper?"

"What do you want?"

"Hmm." She tapped her finger on her chin and

pretended to give it serious consideration. "How about thick steaks, baked potatoes, and fresh peas and carrots."

He stared and then guffawed. "Dream on, lady. How about salt pork and baked potatoes?"

"No peas and carrots?"

He dug into the cupboard and pulled out a tin. "Here you go."

"Canned peas? How lovely." She let out a longsuffering sigh. "However, it is far short of what you offered me."

"I offered you? When did I do that?"

"Didn't you ask what I wanted? I assumed that meant you would provide it. I am sorely disappointed." They grinned at each other.

"Salt pork and canned peas, it is," she said with a flourish.

"Don't forget the baked potatoes." He pulled two nicely shaped potatoes from the sack in the corner cupboard and scrubbed them. He paused as he reached for the oven door. "Can I open it now?"

She sniffed. "Smells like it's done. Open the door carefully and check it." She showed him how to touch the surface and judge if it bounced back. "It's done. Set it to cool."

He did so then stuck the potatoes in to bake.

An hour later, the square of white at the window had darkened to black as they sat at the table and enjoyed the meal.

"Excellent cake," she said after tasting it. "Couldn't have done better myself."

He paused with a forkful of his baking. "I can't believe I did this. Here's hoping I can do it again in the future."

They lingered over seconds of the cake. As they ate, they talked about favorite foods, food disasters, both of their attempts at learning to cook, and various other things.

Flora couldn't believe how comfortable she had grown with this man. In fact, he didn't seem the least bit like the Kade Thomas she had pictured just a few days ago.

The reality of that truth struck her with such a force that she gasped.

How would she react to Kade the next time she saw him in town? Wouldn't Pa notice a difference? How would she explain her change of attitude? If she didn't have a reasonable answer for it, wouldn't Pa become suspicious?

* * *

"WHAT'S WRONG?" Kade asked. "Did you hear something?" He glanced at the door, but the bar was firmly in place. No intruders would be getting in.

"Just a passing thought," she murmured. "Nothing of any interest." She jumped from the table and grabbed the used dishes.

He rose more slowly, wondering at this sudden flurry of action.

"Another night stranded," she said.

Ah, that explained it. Of course, she was anxious about being out another night. "Sorry. I can't make the storm stop."

"My family will be so worried." She held up a hand.

"And don't tell me I should have thought of that before I rode out."

"It didn't cross my mind." And it hadn't. He had learned a new appreciation of her free spirit. "We are only doing the best we can under the circumstances." "I know."

She grew thoughtful. "I hate to make the others worry, especially Ma. I think I have always been a trial to her. I remember being taken to the preacher's house after my mama died. Eve cried and was comforted. I kept trying to run away. I suppose I wanted to find my mama. I don't recall. I only remember the need to run. I can't really explain it, but I had the feeling I was missing something and I had to find it. Ma held me and sang to me for a long time. She says it was three days and three nights before I calmed down. Or maybe I was overcome with exhaustion. Ma's words started to sink into my heart. 'You're safe here. You will always be safe with us. This is your home now. You don't need to run'. I know I am loved and am safe. But sometimes I feel like there is something I have to find."

"What are you looking for?"

"I don't know. Maybe if I did, I could find it." She turned her face toward him. "Do you think it has anything to do with the dreams that waken me?"

"Do you?"

She shrugged. "Maybe I'm just crazy and my mind is unstable."

He laughed outright. "You might be a little wild."

Her eyebrows went up.

"And a little unconventional."

She planted her hands on her hips, silently daring him to say anything more.

He eased back a few inches. "And someone who kicks against the rules of society."

Every bit of warning and displeasure fled from her stance. "I don't mind rules that make sense, but some just don't."

"I'd have to agree." Like forcing a man and woman to marry just because they'd found shelter together against a storm.

They did the dishes and put away the food.

"We can have chocolate cake for breakfast," he said.

She stared at him. "Why Kade Thomas, I never expected to hear such rash words from you."

"How is that rash?"

"It's not what a person has for breakfast. I mean, what would people say?" She pressed her fingers to her mouth and widened her eyes as if shocked.

He chuckled. "I think they would say I was fortunate to have the choice." Even as he spoke, he knew he had voiced a truth that applied to her as well. "I know what you're doing with this conversation."

"Good. A person should have a few choices."

He wasn't going to argue, because they both knew that some things like eating cake were harmless choices while others carried risks not worth taking. All it took to reinforce that fact was a glance at the bookshelf with the reminders.

She followed his gaze. "Seems a shame not to use your new Bible." She went and picked it up. "Why don't you sit here and read it aloud?" She indicated the soft reading chair.

Before he could argue, she drew a kitchen chair close and sat down, waiting for him to take his place.

He sat and took the Bible. "What should I read?"

"Do you have a favorite passage?"

"Can't say as I do. Do you?"

"Genesis chapter twenty-four," she said without hesitation.

He turned the pages and read aloud the story of Abraham's servant going to find a wife for Isaac. He finished and looked at her. "A love story."

"Don't sound surprised. It's a good love story."

"How's that?"

"Because Rebekah was taking care of the camels. That's how the servant knew she was the right woman for Isaac. She wasn't sitting around the house doing needlework. And Isaac loved her."

Kade watched Flora's cheeks grow rosy and knew that this story had deep significance for her. He understood she wanted to be accepted as she was and loved as Isaac loved Rebekah.

"Have you never had a beau?" he asked, imagining a steady line up of admirers.

"I'm seventeen years old. There's plenty of time for that."

"Lots of women are married by your age."

"I suppose that's true. I did have a fondness for a boy back in Ohio. Baron was his name. But when he heard we were moving he lost interest. He was courting another gal before we left. It's of little matter to me. If he could so easily forget me, I can just as easily forget him. Besides..." She ducked her head as if interested in the way her trousers folded at her knees.

"Besides, what?"

Her head came up. "I have this red hair." She tugged at her untidy braid.

Kade studied her hair, his gaze sweeping up one side of her face and down the other. "It's very eye catching."

She narrowed her eyes. "But then, so is a fire."

"Fires keep us warm and cook our food."

"My hair doesn't."

He heard the longing in her voice. "You remember how good the chocolate cake tasted?"

She blinked. "Sure."

He couldn't remember how he meant to turn that into a compliment about her hair. "All I'm saying is that some things are meant to be enjoyed."

Her mouth opened and closed. She pulled her braid forward and looked at it. "I'm afraid this isn't chocolate cake." But she sounded less annoyed at her hair color.

Before he could comment she flipped the braid to her back and fired a question at him. "What about the girl you meant to marry? What happened to her?"

"Well, I was young and idealistic—"

"How young?"

"Nineteen. She was the same age."

"How long ago was that?"

"Three years."

"Oh." She sat back. "So tell me about her."

"There's not much to say. I left to work at a ranch, and when I returned, she had run off with another man."

"You mean she eloped?"

"I don't know if she married him or not. I left the area with my pride in tatters."

"Your pride." She spat the words out. "I'd think if you

74

cared a fig about her you would have gone after her. At least made sure she went of her own accord."

"She left me a note saying adventure called and that she wasn't interested in the dull life I had planned."

"Humph. Didn't she know you were going to go ranching in Montana Territory? Seems that would be enough adventure for her."

He had never thought to hear such words from her. He realized his mouth hung open and he closed it. "A Montana ranch would be enough adventure for you?"

"Well sure, if I was allowed to help with the horses and calves and not be expected to stay in the house all the time." Her eyes grew dreamy. "I'd like to train young colts and help herd cows. I love riding."

"What about babies? Wouldn't you want some of those?"

"I never thought I would until I held Adele's baby. Now I think I'd like to have my own." Her cheeks blossomed again.

"You figure to ride with your babies?" He could almost picture it and grinned.

"A person might have to take turns doing them." Her gaze returned to his, full of challenge.

In spite of himself, he nodded. "A person could do that, I suppose."

She studied him a full minute. He held her gaze, somehow knowing she was assessing him. When she finally nodded, he understood he had passed some sort of test and grinned, his heart releasing a burst of energy.

"Do you go to church regularly?" she asked.

It kept him alert to follow her sudden switches of conversation. "Pretty hard to go when you're on the

Santa Fe Trail or riding herd on cows moving north, but if I'm near a town with a church, I try and go. I remember one trip on the Santa Fe Trail when a preacher traveled with us. I liked how he talked about God and His care and guidance. It made me feel good. Safe. One thing I decided was, when I settled down in my own home, I was going to make it a Christian home. I bought a Bible in New Mexico when I courted Pearl. Thought it was time to start living my plans." His voice trailed off.

"You have the Bible and you have your home."

"But I don't have a family."

"Kade, that is so sad." She brightened. "Tell you what. You can share my family."

He stared at her. "I'm a little too old to be adopted," he said after a bit.

She laughed. "If Ma hears you can bake and ice a chocolate cake, she'll adopt you on the spot." She put her hand over his. "You'd always be welcome."

He looked at their hands. It would be nice to be part of their warmhearted family. He'd already been offered a sincere invitation to come back anytime.

Hearing it from Flora made it more appealing.

But that wasn't what he wanted.

He wanted his own family. Someone to greet him when he came through the door each day. Maybe even someone who shared his interest in ranching.

Not being one to dwell on dreams, he pushed the thoughts aside.

CHAPTER 7

Flora stiffened as she wakened. What had disturbed her sleep? Had she called out from another dream? Or had someone rattled the door? She strained into the silent darkness to hear the sound repeated.

"The wind has gone down," she whispered.

Kade's voice came from the other room. "The storm is over but it's several hours until light. Go back to sleep."

"Yes, sir."

Her briskness earned her a chuckle and she grinned as she turned over. She wakened some time later to the sound of wood being put into the stove. It was still dark though she detected a grayness at the window that indicated dawn.

Kade lit a lamp and Flora hurried to the stove to get warm.

"It's clear out." He smiled down at her.

"I'll be able to get back home today." It wasn't unbridled joy that filled her. "Today I will face Pa and have to explain where I spent the last two days." They looked at each other, silently acknowledging their lives were about to change drastically if she couldn't make her father believe something other than that she had spent two nights with a man she wasn't married to.

With a mixture of sober thought and joyful anticipation, she pulled a saucepan from the cupboard. "You want oatmeal porridge for breakfast?"

"I'm having chocolate cake." He took the pot from her and returned it to the cupboard. "And so are you."

She grinned at him. "I fear I have been a bad influence on you."

He gave a playful jab of his fist to her chin. "It's been an unforgettable couple of days. First, a feisty redheaded woman bangs on my door. Then I beat her at checkers—"

She crossed her arms and pretended to be dismayed. "Don't rub it in."

"Then a crazy man barges into the house."

A shudder crossed her shoulders. "He called himself Eagle Pete and said he could track anything."

"Let's hope he's made tracks so far south we never hear from him again." Kade caught her shoulder. "Please don't give him an opportunity to catch you unawares." His eyes were dark, full of concern, and she was almost ready to promise him anything he asked.

But he laughed. "And I learned to make a chocolate cake. I'd say it's been a good two days."

He said it with a hefty dose of approval that made Flora's insides glow.

The coffee she'd put to brew, boiled, and she grabbed it with her hand wrapped in a towel. She filled two cups as Kade served generous portions of cake, accompanied her to the table, and sat across from her.

"Breakfast is served." The idea of this being breakfast struck her as so odd that she laughed.

He leaned back. "I have to say, cake and coffee make a fine breakfast."

She quirked her eyebrows. "Even if unconventional?"

"Yup. And don't point out how some rules—like cake isn't for breakfast—are silly."

Did he agree that many other man-made rules were unnecessary?

He must have read her mind, for he sat forward and tapped her fingers. "You've taught me a lot."

She didn't ask him to elaborate. It was enough that he'd learned from her.

Pink filled the window and they stood to watch the sunrise.

"The snow is deep," Kade observed.

"I'll take my time." She might have to lead Dollar if his foot was still tender.

They lingered at the window a few more minutes and then turned their attention to cleaning the kitchen.

"I'll take that," he said, when she looked for a place to put the little bit of cake that was left. "I'll have it with coffee later."

"You'll have your house back to yourself." She wondered if he would miss her company.

"It will be quiet." A beat of silence in which she tried to decide if he meant that was a good thing or not. "Too quiet." His voice was so low she wondered if she imagined his words. She glanced at him out of the corner of her eyes.

At the way he studied her, she faced him full on. "You saying you'll miss my company?"

"Guess I am." He grinned. "I enjoyed playing checkers and talking."

"Maybe I'll visit again." She meant to be teasing, but a huge part of her wished she could. Seeing the protest building in his eyes, she held up her hand. "I know. It wouldn't be proper, and goodness knows, we should be proper." She gave a little sniff. "Though I have to ask, how proper is it to eat cake for breakfast?"

When he laughed, she relaxed. No need for him to think she was serious about wanting to visit again.

The dishes were washed and put away. He pulled on his heavy outerwear. She did the same, stopping for one last look around the room before she stepped out into the snow and followed him as he shoveled a path to the barn.

It gave her plenty of time to study her surroundings. The barn was medium-sized and solid red except for white trim at the windows and door. Several smaller buildings created a chain from the house to the barn. Like he said, he'd planned the layout for maximum safety and security through all sorts of weather.

She studied the opening between each building for fear Eagle Pete would jump out. She would have crowded closer to Kade's back except she didn't wish to have his elbow in her face as he scooped aside the snow.

They reached the barn and she hung back until Kade went inside.

He turned and saw her hesitation. "You think that man might have hung around?"

"I don't aim to walk into him if I can avoid it."

"I'm sure he's gone, but I'll have a good look if it will make you feel better." He walked down the alleyway, looking into each pen, and returned. "Nothing here but you, me, and a couple of horses."

"Good. I know I'm being unreasonably fearful, but that man was loathsome."

"You're wise to be careful where someone like him is concerned."

She waited, expecting a lecture on the risks she'd taken that had led her to this situation. But he started saddling his horse without further comment. Nice of him.

"I can make it to town on my own," she said, even though she welcomed his company. Eagle Pete would hesitate to accost her if Kade rode with her, but she didn't want to put Kade out.

"I expect you could, but I don't intend to leave you until we're in sight of Glory. Then I'll hang back so no one will see me and jump to the conclusion that we... well. You know."

"Yeah. I know. Today will be reckoning day with Pa. I won't lie, but he doesn't need to know every detail." She went to Dollar and checked his hoof, then led him up and down the alleyway. "His foot seems healed, but I'll have to take it easy."

She retrieved the saddle blanket and saddle and got Dollar ready to ride while Kade did the same with his big mostly black horse.

"Nice strong-looking animal," she said.

Kade pulled his horse toward her. "Flora, I'd like you to meet Blaze."

She chuckled. "Could it be that you named him that because of the white blaze on his head?"

"A white blaze? You're certain?" Kade pretended surprise and came 'round to stare at his horse. He grinned at Flora and they both laughed.

Leading their horses, they left the barn. Kade paused to close the doors then swung into the saddle.

She swung to Dollar's back, sighed her pleasure, and looked around the place again. "Nice set of corrals," she said, taking in the solid pen with the sturdy post in the center. "See you plan to train horses."

He kept his attention on the snow-covered path. "I'll break trail. It will be easier on your horse if you follow." They set out. "Yes, I plan to break and sell horses."

The snow near the buildings was piled into knee-deep drifts. But in a few minutes, they reached a windswept area that made riding easier. She edged her mount closer.

"I broke Dollar." She patted her horse's neck so Kade would understand who she meant. "Pa bought him from a farmer who had lost most everything. Called him a pity buy because he was unbroken and bad tempered. Pa meant to sell him again, but no one wanted him. I started working with him. Gentle and slow. And now look at him. Pa sort of gave him to me."

Kade turned. "Sort of?"

She grinned. "When he said he was selling him, I cried so hard that Pa said we'd keep him. Pa has his own horse, so mostly Dollar is mine."

"Mostly yours, huh?"

"Yup." With a satisfied smile she looked about. The

sun was bright and brittle. The snow a thousand flashing pinpricks of light.

A house lay to her right, off the road enough she couldn't see any signs of activity. "Who lives there?"

Kade had reined up to look at the place. "The widow Norwood. Her husband died a year or so ago and she's been hanging on to the homestead. I guess she has no other place to go."

Flora had heard about the unfortunate woman. Pa had ridden out with food and clothing on several occasions and expressed his concern for her situation.

"Doesn't she have two little children?"

"She does. I check on her from time to time. I wonder how she fared through the storm."

They continued to watch the place. Flora wasn't comfortable thinking of the woman alone with her little ones. "There isn't any sign of smoke. We better ride in on them."

Together they turned aside. Flora fell back, letting Kade break a trail through the deeper snow. So, he'd been visiting the Widow Norwood, had he? She tried to remember what Pa said about her. Seems she was fairly young. Perhaps Kade had an interest in her. She could provide him with a ready-made family. Just what he needed.

She pushed aside her thoughts as they approached the house and dismounted. "It doesn't feel right to me. No one has been out since it stopped snowing."

"Perhaps she laid in a good store."

"You sound doubtful."

"Or she could have moved into town like people have been telling her to."

"One way to find out." Flora took a step forward then hesitated. "Maybe you should go first. They'll know you better."

"Me? I've barely spoken to the woman. I only check to make sure she has a supply of wood on hand and the pump is working. You're a woman, you go first."

They stood side by side at the door. Flora knocked. And waited. They both bent an ear to the door and listened. Not a sound.

Flora straightened. "I guess it's like you said. They've gone elsewhere." But she couldn't leave without checking. She tried the handle. It turned easily and the door opened. She shivered and hung back as a rancid smell greeted her. Soiled baby diapers or spilled slop pail. The house was cold.

Kade eased by her and she followed. "Oh no." A cot had been pulled close to the stove though the fire had long ago gone out. On the cot lay a woman with two children clutched to her side. Their eyes were closed. "They look—"

She couldn't finish but forced herself to draw closer. From years of helping Ma take care of the ill, injured, and deceased, she knew what to do. She touched each cheek. Cold. But then, the room was like the pit of winter. The widow's eyelids fluttered.

"I prayed help would come." Her whisper was barely audible. "My babies?" She tried to lift her head but lacked the strength.

Kade was at Flora's side. "Keep them covered while I get the fire going." He soon had the stove filled with blazing wood and hurried out to get water. The little girl whimpered. The boy hadn't stirred. She took them to be about three and five respectively. She shook the boy gently, relieved when he protested. Her eyes stung to see their condition but there was no time to dwell on it. They had to be cared for.

"We need lots of hot water," she told Kade.

"I've got some heating already. What else?"

"Tea, something to make a broth with."

He opened cupboards, sending her a shocked look at how bare they were.

"We'll make do with what we can find." She offered them water to drink, relieved that they all took some.

Next was tending to their bodies. She couldn't manage all three at once. The little girl was likely the most vulnerable. She wrapped the boy in a blanket and Kade held him as she turned her attention to the younger child.

She took off the soiled clothing and tossed it into a corner to deal with later and gently sponged her clean. She had sores on her bottom that would heal with proper care.

Widow Norwood watched with eyes full of sorrow. "I did the best I could."

"I know. How long have you been sick?"

"I don't know."

Flora knew from the odor that the woman had vomited. She guessed the children had suffered from the grippe too, and with no one to tend to them, they had grown weak and unable to help themselves.

The little one was clean. "I'm going to get something for her to wear."

The widow's gaze went to the door past the kitchen and Flora hurried to the small bedroom and searched the drawers. They had so little that it made Flora's insides ache. She found a woolen dress for the little girl and recognized it as one Ma had sewn out of an old garment given to them. With stockings and a sweater, the child would be warm. She found clothing for the boy and the mother and returned to the kitchen. She dressed the girl and then gave her to Kade to hold. The little one's eyes widened at being plunked on this stranger's knees.

Flora bent over. "He's a good man. He won't hurt you. Rest here while I take care of your brother and your mother."

Flora looked into Kade's eyes and saw the same determination she felt. They would do everything in their power to help this small family. He gave a little smile that went a long way to easing her concern.

The boy wasn't as cooperative as his sister. He curled into a ball and resisted her as she removed his soiled clothing.

"Donny, let the lady help you," the mother said in a voice so weak it might have been a summer wind passing through the house.

Donny whined and continued to fight her, but Flora gently washed him and dressed him, all the time talking. "You're okay. You're safe. We're going to help you." As she spoke, she realized she used the same words Ma had used to comfort her when she had come to the Kinsley family.

The children were cleaned and looking a little more alert.

"Now for mama," Flora said.

"Please feed my babies first."

Flora looked at Kade, silently begging him for a way to feed them.

"Cellar," Widow Norwood said.

Flora looked around and saw the trap door by the table.

Kade saw it too. "I'll go down." He set the girl on the chair, wrapped her in a blanket.

They all watched as he lifted the door and disappeared under the house. A light flared and she guessed he'd found a candle down there. "Got a few things." He reemerged and held up a pint of bottled meat, three limp carrots, and two small potatoes.

Flora almost cheered. "We'll get some soup into all three of you soon, and before long you'll be feeling better."

While she poured the meat into a large pot and added water to create a thin broth, Kade peeled the potatoes and carrots.

"They should be shredded," Flora said. But a search of the cupboards didn't reveal a shredder of any sort.

"I'll scrape them." Kade took the sharp knife and did so.

The mixture came to a boil and she let it simmer. "Mrs. Norwood, I need to clean you up, but I can't provide the privacy I know you will want."

"I'll fix that." Kade arranged the chairs in a line and hung blankets over them. "I'll keep the children over there." He pointed to the far corner and took the last chair there. He sat with his back to the women, gently bouncing the children on his knees. Neither child had the energy to protest or struggle.

Flora smiled at the sweet picture the three of them made then turned her attention to the sick woman. She was all bones and loose flesh as if she'd been sick some time. Or perhaps she had starved herself, so the children had enough to eat. Flora clamped her teeth together. Just as soon as the widow was strong enough to move, Flora would see she got into town and was properly looked after.

By the time she had the woman in a clean garment and fresh bedding on the bed, the soup was ready. She dipped off some of the broth and diluted it for the children. Kade returned to the kitchen area and the five of them clustered close to the stove.

Flora held the cup of broth for the little girl. "What's her name?" she asked the mother.

"Blossom."

That brought a smile to Flora's lips. It was a perfect name for a child with golden blond hair and dark blue eyes.

Meanwhile, Kade held the cup for Donny and he drank the broth, his dark eyes guarded at these strangers taking over his home. The boy was like his mother with brown hair and brown eyes.

As soon as Blossom finished, Flora helped the mother lift her head and held a cup to her lips. She took three swallows, then fell back exhausted.

The children, too, were weary and climbed up beside their mama.

Flora covered them, then signaled Kade to follow her to the far corner. "They are very weak. I don't know…" She shook her head.

Kade squeezed her shoulder. "We will do all we can to help and pray that God will see fit to bring them back to health and strength."

She nodded, fighting an urge to lean against his chest.

"I can't help thinking this is so much like what I went through. I was older than Blossom but younger than Donny when my mother died in rather similar circumstances. I don't remember it much, but Eve certainly does. She says our mama died and we were all alone, hungry and afraid until neighbors found us and took us to the Kinsley's." Shivers raced through her.

Kade caught her shoulders and turned her so he could look into her eyes. "Like your ma said, you're safe now."

She nodded. "I know, but sometimes I feel afraid and I don't even know why."

He dipped his head to touch her forehead.

She drank in the strength and comfort his presence offered. "I'm so glad you're with me. I don't know if I could handle this alone."

"You could. I think you can handle whatever crosses your path."

She gave a little laugh. "Maybe not an angry skunk."

They both laughed and stepped apart.

"What do we need to do?" he asked.

"Give them fluids and small amounts of weakened broth until we're sure their stomachs can handle it."

"Should we waken them?"

Flora tried to think how Ma would handle this situation. "Let them rest for an hour, then we'll give them something."

He pulled two chairs into the corner and they sat together, talking softly as the minutes passed. He didn't suggest leaving, and she was grateful. She didn't know where her fear came from; she only knew it wasn't as gripping when he was near.

CHAPTER 8

Kade's opinion of Flora had undergone a complete transformation. This wild rebel was a capable, caring young woman. She handled the situation calmly despite her fears.

He knew the family, especially the mother, was near the point of death when he and Flora found them. The mother still hovered too close for his peace of mind.

He vowed he would not leave Flora to handle this on her own. Yes, her family would be beside themselves with worry, but they'd understand and forgive her when they learned what she'd done.

They talked quietly as they waited to waken the family for more nourishment.

He told her stories about being on the Santa Fe Trail.

"You could write a book," she said, laughing at his description of one of the camp dogs.

"Never thought of it."

She chuckled. "And you don't intend to think about it either, do you?"

"I'm not much good with pen and paper. I never went to school, though Pa made sure we could read and write. Mostly he made sure we could cipher really well."

"You read well too." Her smile landed in his heart with a gentleness that left him feeling blessed.

They had shared a few special moments in the past couple of days. Maybe his home wouldn't seem so lonely now.

Or would it feel even lonelier? Not a pleasant prospect.

She got to her feet. "We should waken them."

He followed her across the room. "What do you want to give them?"

"Weak tea. Too bad there isn't any sugar."

He prepared the tea as she wakened the children.

Donny sat up. "I'm hungry."

"Glad to hear it," Flora said. "Have some tea, and if your stomach feels okay, you can have soup."

He refused to let Kade hold the cup and drank the tea in large, noisy gulps, then held out the cup. "I'm feeling good. I'll have soup, please."

Flora laughed. "Let me take care of your sister first." She held the cup to Blossom's mouth. The child drank slowly, her big eyes going from Flora to Kade and back as if making sure both remained in her sight and didn't do anything scary.

Blossom finished and lay down beside her mama again.

Flora dipped out some broth for Donny and he drank it eagerly.

Flora grinned at Kade. "Seems he's on the mend." She

turned to Blossom. "Honey, why don't you sit on Kade's lap while I help your mama?"

Blossom gave them both a wide-eyed blue stare.

"He's a nice man. Did you know he lives nearby?"

"I've come by and chopped wood for your mama a time or two." Kade hoped his quiet voice was enough to calm both Flora's fears and Blossom's.

The child studied Kade then sat up and held out her arms. "Okay, I go."

Flora lifted her to Kade, and he held both children as Flora wakened their mother with a gentleness that touched a spot deep in Kade's heart. He'd not known cruelty in his life, but his memory of a woman's touch was very dim.

"How are you feeling?" Flora asked. "Any pains in your stomach?"

"No pains." The sick woman's voice was breathless, as if it took too much energy to answer.

"Would you like to try some tea?"

"Please."

Flora helped Mrs. Norwood sit up and held a cup to her lips.

"Good." The cup was empty, and Flora smiled at Kade.

Mrs. Norwood lay down, spent by the effort of drinking. Blossom scrambled from Kade's lap and crawled up beside her mama. The two of them appeared to sleep.

Donny sat cross-legged on a chair, studying Kade. "You a cowboy?" he asked.

"I guess you could call me that."

"You ever been bucked off a horse?"

Kade chuckled, glancing at Flora and sharing a moment of amusement. "A time or two," he admitted.

"Then I guess you ain't much of a cowboy." Little Donny sounded so disgusted that Kade laughed, keeping his voice low so he didn't disturb the sleeping pair.

Flora's eyes sparkled with humor.

He would like to know what she was thinking.

Donny shifted his attention to Flora. "How come your hair is red?"

She crossed her arms and tilted her head back and forth, studying his hair. "How come yours is brown?"

"I was born that way."

"Me too."

"Oh. It isn't 'cause you got burned or anything?"

Kade looked from the boy to Flora, wondering if she knew what Donny meant.

Flora blinked. "Why would you say that?"

"Your hair is the color of fire, is all."

Flora chuckled. "No, Donny. I haven't been on fire."

"Okay." He shifted to look at his mother and sister. "Mama is awfully sick, ain't she?"

Flora took the boy in her arms and sat holding him. "She is, but we're going to help all of you get better."

"Mama prayed someone would come help us." He twisted to look at Flora. "Are you an angel? Do angels have fire-colored hair?"

"I'm not an angel."

Kade chuckled at the dry tone of her words. "You sure?" he teased, thinking how she had blessed his home with laughter and companionship for a couple of days and how she'd efficiently tended this poor family.

She met his gaze, holding it with an intensity he

couldn't release himself from. "Are you sure you're the same man who spoke to me of my behavior last week and who greeted me with criticism not very many days ago?"

"I am, but I might have misjudged you to a degree."

"A degree? How generous of you."

"Mama?" Donny slipped from Flora's lap and knelt at the bedside of his mother.

Mrs. Norwood cupped her hand over her son's head. "You're feeling better?"

"Lots better. Are you better?"

"I'm doing all right. In fact, I might like a bit of that broth."

Flora hurried to put some in a cup. She helped the woman sit up and then held it to her mouth. After three swallows, Mrs. Norwood fell back, exhausted.

Flora gave Kade a look brimming with worry and signaled him to the corner where they could talk. "They need to be in town where they can be taken care of better. Ma would tend them. They would have proper food."

"Are they strong enough to make the trip?"

"I believe so. I'm afraid if Mrs. Norwood stays here another day, she will only grow weaker. Can you go to town and ask Pa to come with a wagon?"

Kade caught her shoulders and looked into her blue eyes. "He'll know we've been together through the storm."

"He doesn't have to. This situation provides the perfect explanation. You let it sound like I've been here."

"How do I do that?"

"You could say I'm with the widow, whom you often

check on. I've been taking care of her, but now that the storm is over, she needs to be taken to town."

He considered her words. They were true without revealing the truth. He didn't like to deceive the preacher but neither did he want to be forced into a marriage neither of them wanted.

"That might work. You'll be okay until we get back?" He didn't like to leave her to deal with three sick people, though Donny appeared to be recovering quickly. "I'll make sure you have enough wood and water to last until I get back."

"You won't be more than an hour or two, will you?"

He heard the hint of fear in her voice. "I'll be back as soon as possible. I promise."

He squeezed her hands and held them until determination filled her eyes. Only then did he put on his coat, hat, and mittens. He brought in more wood and filled the water buckets then tended to her horse before he rode for town. The trail was clear, which made for easy riding.

He turned to look back at the house. *Lord, keep them safe.* Then he was on his way.

Would the preacher believe the half-truth he meant to tell?

* * *

FLORA WATCHED out the window until she could no longer see Kade, then she turned away.

She was alone with a very ill woman and her children. At least Donny seemed improved. Work was the best way to make the hours pass quickly. She filled a basin with hot soapy water and washed the table and the cupboards.

Every so often, Mrs. Norwood opened her eyes and watched her. She signaled Flora to come close enough to hear her. "I will clean the place once I have my strength back."

Flora patted her hand. "I know you will, but it helps pass the time if I keep busy."

Mrs. Norwood smiled. "You're missing your fellow."

"He's not—" How was she going to explain the two of them landing here together? "I barely know the man." Which perhaps wasn't entirely true. "I believe he was checking on you and we both noticed the lack of smoke from the chimney at the same time."

"I see."

Flora wondered how much the woman saw. "Mr. Thomas has gone to town to fetch my father. We'll get you to a warm, safe place. My ma and pa's house to be exact."

"I couldn't...I can't..."

"You need help. Your children need help." She stroked Blossom's head. The child opened her eyes and stared at Flora, pressing to her mama's side.

Mrs. Norwood nodded. "I can't afford to be prideful."

"My pa is the preacher."

"He's a good man." The woman grew weary from talking and Flora slipped away.

After another hour or so she persuaded Blossom to have some broth. Donny eagerly took more. Their mother managed a bit more tea. And then the room was quiet. Donny played with a toy horse at his mother's feet and Blossom cuddled to her sleeping mother's side.

Flora stood at the stove wishing she had something to occupy her hands and her thoughts. She smiled. Something besides remembering how much she had enjoyed the past two days. She'd thought Kade stiff and judgmental. Instead, she'd found him to be warmhearted, kind, amusing, and surprisingly good company.

The door handle rattled. Good, he was back. Pa must be following with a wagon.

The door flew back with a thud.

Eagle Pete filled the entrance. "Told ya I would find ya." He held a gun.

Flora didn't shift her attention from the man. Her coat with the gun in its pocket hung two feet to Eagle Pete's right. There was no way she would be able to get it and force him from the house.

Blossom cried. Donny shifted toward his ma and Mrs. Norwood pulled both her children closer.

Flora stared at the man, her heart twisting with a combination of fear and anger. "Thought you had the good sense to leave here."

"Guess you thought wrong, missee." He drooled as he leered at her.

Mrs. Norwood hushed her children.

Flora did not take her eyes off the intruder as she tried to think what to do. She did not want to put the others in danger, yet she didn't want to move away from the cot and put herself in the open. *Lord, now would be a good time for You to intervene.*

Eagle Pete took a step inside.

"I wouldn't come closer if I was you." She said the first thing that popped into her mind. "Not unless you want smallpox."

Eagle Pete ground to a halt and squinted at the Norwood family. Thankfully, the mother had pulled the blanket around them so he couldn't see enough to judge if Flora spoke the truth or not.

He waved the gun at Flora. "You come over here."

"I've been thoroughly exposed. I don't know how long before I break out in the sores that drain pus and give off a dreadful odor." She sniffed. "I think you can smell it for yourself." Let him think the smell of vomit and other things signaled smallpox.

"I ain't going without you."

She shrugged. "If that's how you feel about it. You ever seen smallpox up close?"

"Stop jawing and get over here."

"I have no intention of going with you."

"Then I'm gonna shoot you." He waved his gun around. "I'm gonna shoot the whole works of you."

"Miss Kinsley." Mrs. Norwood's whisper conveyed her fear.

Flora didn't leave off trying to stare down Eagle Pete. "I can't believe you'd be so low as to shoot innocent children."

"I ain't got no reason not to."

"Perhaps a little compassion." If she could just keep him talking until—

Until what? She didn't want Pa walking into this situation. Eagle Pete would likely shoot him without blinking an eye.

CHAPTER 9

ade saw the horse in the widow's yard before he turned on the trail to the house. Had someone else ridden by and been concerned? Or…

His nerves twitched. Perhaps the visitor was not of a kindly mindset.

Kade dismounted, tied his horse to the nearest fence post, and took a circuitous route to the house, one that would keep him from being seen from the window.

He reached the house and edged around the corner until he could see the door. It stood open, letting in cold air. His nerves twitched. No one would purposely let the house cool off with a sick family inside. He pressed to the wall and eased closer until he could see what was going on.

Eagle Pete. His heart slammed into his ribs. Why hadn't the man left the area? And why was he standing motionless? Did Flora have her gun trained on him?

Kade moved an inch closer. Another inch. The man held a gun. Kade drew back, unable to draw in air.

"Get over here or I'll shoot you dead." Eagle Pete's words dripped with warning and eagerness.

The man was fixated on getting his hands on Flora.

Kade was not about to let that happen.

A piece of firewood lay at Kade's feet. He must have dropped it when he carried wood to the house. He eased down and picked it up, silently closed the distance to the door, coiled his muscles, and leaped forward. Before anyone realized he was there, he crashed the hunk of wood to Eagle Pete's head as hard as he could, knowing it would take a lot to fell the big man.

Eagle Pete grunted and cursed, flung about to see who had attacked him. The gun wavered drunkenly in his hands. His eyes rolled back in his head and he crashed to the floor.

Kade stepped over his body and rushed to Flora. She flew into his arms. "Thank you for showing up when you did."

He held her tight. "Are you hurt? Is anyone hurt?"

"We're fine." She glanced at the unconscious man and shuddered. "Shouldn't we tie him up?"

"Like a trussed turkey." He took the dropped gun and handed it to Flora. "Keep an eye on him while I get some rope." He went to the barn and returned with enough rope to tie the man securely.

All the while Flora stood by, the gun ready.

Kade suspected if the man came to before he was bound hand and foot, she would shoot him before he could decide whether or not to try anything.

When Kade returned and she was sure the man

wouldn't be getting away, she pocketed the gun and laughed. "He's going to start having nightmares about firewood."

Kade grinned. "Might teach him to stay away from other people's houses."

"He might be beyond learning anything useful."

Kade didn't know if she meant she thought he was dead or simply thought the man wasn't capable of putting together how his actions were the cause of his problems.

She let out a shuddering breath. "Is Pa coming?"

"Should be along any minute." Kade glanced out the window. "Here he comes now."

Flora moved to Kade's side. "Did he...you know? Are we out of danger?"

Kade nodded. Though he ached to ask what would be so awful about being married to him.

"I need to pack up their things." She hurried to the bedroom and by the time her father arrived, she had filled a wooden box with belongings to take with the Norwoods.

The preacher drove the wagon up to the door and came in. He looked at the trussed-up man on the floor then hugged Flora. "Praise God you are okay. We were so worried." He went to Mrs. Norwood's side. "Now, Stella, have I not been telling you for weeks that you should be in town? But God was merciful to send my daughter to help you throughout the storm."

"Yes, preacher, the Lord is good." Mrs. Norwood gave Flora a questioning look as if to ask what her pa meant about the storm, but she didn't press the matter.

Kade understood she was too weak right now, but

once she regained her strength, would she clear up the confusion?

The preacher touched the heads of the two little ones and they smiled at him.

"Now, someone better explain who this is." The preacher stared at Eagle Pete, who picked that moment to open his eyes and groan.

"You hit me from behind. That ain't fair." His eyes didn't focus as he looked at two men.

"Pa, this man followed me. Twice he tried to force me to go with him."

Eagle Pete rolled his eyes. "Should know better than to go after a redhead."

The preacher nudged the man's boots. "You better think twice about going after any of my daughters in the future." A brief pause. "Or any young woman within riding distance." He turned his back on the man. "Now let's get everyone to town."

"Pa, what about him?" Flora tipped her head toward Eagle Pete. "Can we just leave him here?"

Kade smiled at the eagerness in her voice.

"He can go visit the sheriff. I'm sure he'll find the jail cell to his liking."

Kade felt the cold in the preacher's voice. Knew he didn't take kindly to anyone threatening his daughters in any way. Like spending two unchaperoned nights with one of them. Kade did not dare look at Flora for fear his glance would give away his worry that her pa might learn the truth and be angry. No doubt he would see it as a righteous anger.

He dragged Eagle Pete out of the way then helped the preacher carry out the Norwood belongings. Mrs.

Kinsley had made a bed in the wagon and sent along an abundance of blankets and quilts. Kade carried Mrs. Norwood out and made sure she was well wrapped. The preacher and Flora each carried a child and bundled them up beside their mother.

Kade went back in and made sure the fire in the stove was low enough not to be a danger. His arms akimbo, he looked down at Eagle Pete. "I suppose we could leave him here and send the sheriff to get him." "I'll freeze," the man whined.

The preacher grabbed one of Eagle Pete's arms and waved Kade forward. "Help him to his feet. We'll put him on his horse, and he can follow along."

Flora brought Kade's horse and led her own but didn't offer to get Eagle Pete's horse.

"Flora, bring his horse to the door."

She looked ready to defy her father, then with a long-suffering sigh led the horse to her pa. "If I had my way, I'd tie a rope from his neck to the wagon and make him walk all the way."

"Daughter, we don't let our emotions direct our actions."

"Yes, Pa." She stood a good ways off as Kade and the preacher struggled to get Eagle Pete into the saddle and tie him so he wouldn't escape.

"My head hurts," the big man complained.

No one offered him the least bit of sympathy.

"You folks sure don't act like good Christian people should."

Kade choked back his laughter at the look of rage on Flora's face. She patted her pocket and he knew she contemplated shooting the man. Kade edged closer to her. "I'm thinking your thoughts are lacking in Christian virtue."

"You'd be right. Do you know he was prepared to shoot us all? Even the children. In my opinion, the man deserves to hang."

Her pa overheard her and spoke gently. "None of us deserve mercy, and yet we are recipients of it every day."

Flora got into the saddle without answering.

Kade did the same and they rode on either side of the wagon with Eagle Pete's horse securely tied beside Flora's pa. Kade thought they made a strange procession and mostly a silent one except for Eagle Pete's endless complaints about the unfairness of his situation and how his head hurt.

They reached Glory. Several curtains were pushed aside to watch them pass. No doubt the rumors would be flying before they even unloaded the wagon.

They made their way to the two-story house beside the church. Preacher Kinsley had built the house according to his specifications. Kade had been inside twice at Mrs. Kinsley's invitation to join the family for after-church dinner. From what he'd seen, there was a kitchen and dining room combined that was big enough to seat a couple dozen people. A hall led to a quiet parlor. He'd glimpsed some bedrooms off the hall but couldn't say how many. Mostly he wanted to eat the food set before him, which was delicious, and get away from the way the other cowboys stared at or flirted with the Kinsley girls.

A young lad ran beside the wagon. "Preacher, you got a prisoner? What'd he do?"

"Jimmy, you run and get the sheriff," the preacher said.

"Can't. He rode out of town this morning and ain't come back yet."

"Thanks for the information. Guess we'll keep him with us a bit longer."

Kade glanced at Flora across the wagon and grinned at the way she scowled at Eagle Pete. The man didn't realize how close he came to being shot for his actions.

They reached the manse and Mrs. Kinsley rushed out to the back of the wagon, her blonde hair fading to white in a tidy bun. "Stella, my dear, how are you and the little ones?"

"I've been better." Mrs. Norwood sounded wearier than when they'd left.

Flora jumped to the ground and faced her mother. Flora was several inches taller than Mrs. Kinsley, but the look in the older woman's blue eyes was steady and demanding. She took a good look at the trousers her daughter wore. "Flora, look at you," she scolded, then pulled the girl into a long hug. "I'm so glad you're okay. It was good you stumbled upon Stella and could stay with her through the storm. That was advantageous for both of you."

"What?" Eagle Pete roared. "Who said she stayed with that woman? I found her in his house." He tipped his head toward Kade. "Think you can get away with stealing her from me, do ya?"

Kade's heart hit bottom with a thud that made the soles of his feet hurt. He stood beside the wagon feeling the sting of the preacher's look, hearing her mother gasp, and feeling most unmerciful toward Eagle Pete.

"Is that true?" The preacher's voice left no doubt as to his anger.

Kade met the preacher's look squarely, not letting the piercing gray eyes make him quiver. "It is true."

"I hope you planned to tell me."

Kade held his head high. "No sir. I did not."

The preacher roared. "You care nothing about my daughter's reputation?"

Three girls crowded together in the open doorway, eager to hear what was going on.

Kade saw them out of the corner of his eyes, but his attention was riveted to the preacher.

"Pa, I asked him not to." Flora gave her father a look that made Kade remember why he called her the rebel. "I knew you'd be angry and want to force us to marry."

"That's right. We'll get the Norwoods settled and taken care of. I'll personally lock this man in jail and then…" He yanked his hat from his head, revealing dark brown hair with just a hint of gray at the temples. "Then we are going to have a wedding." His look dared Flora to argue then he fixed Kade with a blaze of challenge. "And if you aren't here, I will hunt you down. So, get ready for your wedding day."

* * *

FLORA FOLLOWED THE ENTOURAGE INSIDE. Pa carried Mrs. Norwood—Stella. Ma carried Blossom, but Donny insisted he could walk. Kade helped Eagle Pete as far as the door then indicated he should remain there. Kade said something to the man but she didn't hear what.

Eagle Pete sank to the floor. "Don't blame me 'cause I told the truth."

Flora's sisters crowded around her asking what happened. Did Eagle Pete really threaten her and had she truly spent two days—and nights —with Kade?

"He's very handsome," Josie said.

"I kept telling you not to act so wild," Eve whispered.

Flora did her best to ignore them as her mind raced down one trail and then another seeking an escape from Pa's edict that she and Kade marry.

She paused in the hallway. Perhaps she could slip out the back door and disappear.

But Ma emerged from the bedroom where Stella and Blossom had been taken. "Flora, you go on upstairs and change into something decent."

Eagle Pete snorted amusement.

Flora scowled at him and patted the pocket of her trousers. "Still got my gun."

"Flora." Ma sounded shocked. "Are you threatening to shoot a man? In the manse. Lord, have mercy."

"Mercy? For him but not for me?"

"I'll take the gun." Kade held out his hand.

"I'm sorry." She meant because he was being forced to marry her. She couldn't say what he was thinking, but the way he held her gaze eased away some of the tension tightening her insides. She handed him the gun.

"Don't hesitate to shoot him if he tries to escape."

"You are a vicious gal," Eagle Pete groused. "Guess I should be happy poor Kade is going to be stuck with you."

Flora kicked his booted foot. "Lucky you." Flora marched toward the stairs.

"Do something with your hair," Ma called.

Flora yanked the tie from her untidy braid and shook her hair, knowing it would be a wild tangle of curls.

"Now it really looks like she's on fire," Donny said.

It perfectly described how Flora felt. She would not marry a man who didn't love her. But how was she to persuade Pa?

She continued up the stairs. Eve followed her into the bedroom they shared though all that separated them from the others in the open area was a curtain. Not that Flora minded. Her sisters were good friends, but at the moment, she could do without Eve's downturned mouth. She knew before Eve spoke that she would scold her.

"How many times have I warned you that your actions would lead to disaster?"

"More times than I care to count. Don't forget to add, *Be sure your sins will find you out,* and, *Every choice taken has a consequence.*"

"I think you're learning the truth of those sayings. Unfortunately, you won't get a chance to change soon enough to avoid a forced marriage."

Flora could think of no reply that didn't sound childish. And she wouldn't let anyone know just how sorry she was to have arrived at this place. She stepped out of her trousers and hung them in the back of the wardrobe, hoping Ma wouldn't remove them. She stared at the dresses and skirts before her.

Eve came to her side. "Better wear your best gown. Too bad there isn't time to make a proper wedding dress." She pulled out a heavy green woolen dress that Flora hated because of how it restricted her movements with its fitted bodice and tight sleeves.

"It itches me." She put it back in the wardrobe and pulled out a sapphire-blue gown made of sateen. "This is my favorite dress."

Eve examined it carefully. "It could do with a sponging. It looks like you dragged the hem in some mud. But I guess it will do." She waited while Flora slipped into it. "Now let's do something with your hair."

Flora rocked her head back and forth, sending waves of red curls about her shoulders. "I'm going to leave it loose. To show that I'm an innocent girl."

"I think you've given Ma enough to deal with. Sit down and I'll fix your hair."

Flora gave in. Ma wasn't the only one who had things to deal with. Flora was expected downstairs in short order to stand beside Kade and become his wife.

"He seems like a nice man," Eve said as she brushed though Flora's curls. The brush caught on a knot. It hurt but Flora knew better than to complain.

"Was it awkward having to stay there? How did you pass the time?"

"He's a good checker player. Better'n me, even."

Eve's hands grew idle. "He beat you?" She took Flora's silence for agreement and chuckled. "I guess he is good then."

After a moment, Flora added, "I taught him to bake a chocolate cake."

"It sounds very cozy and domestic." Eve's voice was low, gentle.

"I know you're trying to make me feel better about being forced to marry him."

"You might as well make the best of it." Eve twisted Flora's hair into a roll around her head and placed hairpins to hold it in place, then, apparently remembering what Flora's hair was like, she added another dozen pins. "There you go. All set for your wedding day."

Wedding day! It sounded like nails in her coffin. "Do you mind giving me a few minutes alone to get ready?"

Eve hugged her. "I'll wait downstairs."

Flora walked the length of the floor and back. She paused to look out the window, but the whole town could have been on fire for all the mind she gave to the scene beyond the glass. Her wedding day? She hadn't given marriage a whole lot of thought, but certainly what little she'd considered had not included marrying someone against his will.

She went to the wardrobe, pulled out the trousers, and began to unbutton her dress. Her hands grew idle. It was impossible to get past everyone downstairs. She returned to the window. If she climbed out...

But Pa must have had her in mind when he built the house. There was nothing between the window and the ground two stories down. And nothing on the ground to cushion her fall. She might break a leg, but Pa wouldn't see that as a reason to delay the wedding longer than it took to get her settled in bed and her leg bound up.

If she was to be forced to marry, she preferred to do it standing on her two feet.

She hung the trousers back in the wardrobe and rebuttoned her dress.

There was only one thing she could do. Pulling in a deep breath that did nothing to ease the way her insides jumped, she opened the door and marched down the stairs.

"You're ready. Good," Pa said. "All of you come along to the parlor."

Flora met Kade's steady gaze and drew courage from it. "Pa, there's something I have to say." Pa didn't appear pleased with her delay.

"I was lost in the storm and stumbled into Kade's house. He was kind enough to shelter me from the storm. He behaved like a gentleman the whole time. Shouldn't you be grateful rather than judging me?"

Eve gasped at Flora's boldness in arguing with their father.

"Daughter, I am not judging. I am protecting you. I believe you when you say nothing inappropriate happened, but not everyone will be so generous. Many a decent man won't want to marry you, and many a scoundrel will think he can take advantage of you."

Several pairs of eyes went to Eagle Pete. He crossed his arms and turned away, his nose in the air.

She couldn't believe he even cared what others thought.

"I'm prepared to do the honorable thing," Kade said. "I'm willing to marry her."

If they'd been alone, she might have been tempted to hug him for being so noble. But the truth was, he had no more desire to marry than did she.

"Let us proceed." Pa took a step toward the parlor.

"Wait. I'm not finished." She widened her eyes so she wouldn't reveal any of the nervousness she felt at what she was going to do. "I believe there is only one reason for marriage, and that is if a man and woman love each other so much they can't imagine living without the other." Her voice grew stronger. "Seeing as that is not the case here, I refuse to marry Kade against my will."

Her sisters and Ma gasped. Pa looked ready to deliver a roar of thunder.

Flora glanced at Kade. Saw a little smile tugging at his lips and took it to mean he was pleased at her refusal to marry him.

Eagle Pete's chuckle broke the stunned silence.

"I'll marry her if Kade doesn't want her."

Flora took a threatening step toward him.

His humor fled. "You should be happy someone will be wanting to marry you after they hear you spent two nights with that fella. Not everyone is as forgivin' as me."

"You will marry him," Pa roared. "It isn't up for discussion."

Her insides shook like she'd swallowed a wind-driven storm but she held her ground, revealing none of her fear.

"No, Pa. I won't."

CHAPTER 10

ade had to admire Flora's brave stubbornness in facing her father and refusing to give in to his orders. It took a lot of guts. He couldn't see the preacher's face but guessed from the set of his shoulders that he meant to win this battle. Flora seemed set on winning too. The stalemate could go on for some time if someone didn't offer a solution. Kade might be the only one present who could.

"Preacher Kinsley, may I speak to you in private?"

The preacher slowly came 'round, his dark gaze boring into Kade.

Kade drew himself up tall and met that insistent gaze without flinching.

A beat of silence in which the whole room waited for the decision.

"Very well." The preacher led the way to the parlor and closed the door. "What do you have to say for yourself?"

Kade knew he must present his case in such a way as

to convince the man. "I'm ready to do what is right by Flora, but I'm sure you know your daughter well enough to know if she is forced to do something she doesn't want to, she will rebel. Give me time to court her properly. Let her learn to care for me so she is willing to marry me." Having spent the past couple days with her, he knew she was good company. He hoped he could make her see that they could do well together.

"Flora doesn't know what's good for her."

"Let me help her see." Though she simply might not like him. In that case—

"Fine. I'll give you two weeks to make her agreeable. Or you will marry her whether or not she likes it. The girl needs to be tamed."

It was on the tip of Kade's tongue to say what she needed was to be loved but he wasn't sure he had the right, nor if he could give her what she needed. But two weeks? What could he hope to accomplish in that span of time?

"Any objections?" the preacher asked. Kade knew he meant there would not be any.

"Two weeks? Fine."

Kade followed the preacher from the parlor. He should have asked the man not to tell Flora of their agreement for fear she would dig in her heels at the idea of being courted in order to change her mind.

The preacher faced his wife and daughters. "The wedding is temporarily postponed." It appeared he knew his daughter well enough to avoid inviting her resistance.

"What?"

"Why?"

Questions barraged the preacher.

He held up his hand. "It's what I have decided."

Flora let out a huge sigh and grinned widely. "Thank you, Pa." She laughed and hugged Eve then each of her sisters.

She paused in front of her mother. "I will help you take care of the Norwoods."

Kade noticed she didn't say she would reform. He grinned. That seemed too much to expect.

Donny looked about the adults. "So, they don't have to get married?"

"Not today," the preacher said. Kade was sure everyone heard the warning in his voice.

"I gotta tell Ma." The boy ran into the bedroom.

"I'm still willing," Eagle Pete said. "I could enjoy living in a house like this." He eyed the room. "Right now, I sure would like to sit in one of them soft chairs."

"I'll take him to the jail," Kade said, and helped Eagle Pete to his feet. Ignoring the man's grumbling, he escorted him to the jail. The sheriff had returned, so Kade gave him the details of the offenses and left the man in the cell. The sheriff said he would be shipped off to trial and the territorial prison. It was a relief to know the man would not again threaten Flora.

He had to return to the manse to get his horse.

Flora must have been watching for him for she ran out before he unhitched Blaze.

"What did you say to Pa?"

He'd known this question was coming and had considered the best way to answer it. There wasn't a doubt in his mind what her reaction would be if she knew his courting was to win her over so she wouldn't angrily enter into marriage. If she ever learned the truth, he hoped she wouldn't have a pistol nearby and that he was far away. "I said you wouldn't take kindly to being forced to wed. Don't think that would lead to a happy union, do you?"

"Most certainly not. But I can't believe that was enough to convince Pa to change his mind. Especially when I had tried unsuccessfully."

Kade grinned down at her. "Guess I'm more persuasive than you are."

The way she squinted at him gave him cause to think she wasn't totally convinced, but it might not hurt for her to be a little uncertain about what lay ahead.

He untied his horse. "I'm going home. Maybe I'll see you around."

"I expect so." Her airy response failed to convince him she wasn't sorry to see him leave. Likely because she would have to face her family alone. Endure her father's wrath and her mother's disappointment. He wished he could stay and help her deal with it all.

"I enjoyed your company," he said, lingering beside his horse. Never before had going back to his empty house seemed difficult.

She stood close to him, rubbing her hand along his mount's neck. "Don't eat chocolate cake for breakfast every day."

He laughed. "No one will know if I do or not."

"Huh. Be sure your sins will find you out." A world of woe filled her words. Perhaps she regretted riding out like she had. The thought vanished as soon as it came. More likely she regretted getting into a situation that required she spend a couple of nights with him. Not that it had been so bad.

"Nothing in the Bible against eating cake."

She laughed. "Then enjoy it."

He took the reins but still didn't swing into the saddle. She would face her father's disapproval and the slanted looks of her sisters and mother on her own. "I hate to leave you to deal with them." He tipped his head toward the house to indicate what he meant.

"I can handle them." Her smile turned her eyes to a blue that matched her dress.

"Nice dress," he murmured. "Looks good on you."

"Why, Kade Thomas, is that you sounding like you approve of me?" She gave a playful punch to his shoulder.

"Ow." He rubbed his arm.

She chuckled. "Poor boy. Did I injure you?" He nodded and tried to look sad.

She laughed. "You're teasing me."

"Uh huh." It surprised him how much he enjoyed doing so. "I have to go."

"I believe you said that already." Yet neither of them moved.

Somewhere a door slammed. He couldn't have said if it was the front door of the manse a few feet away or a more distant house, but it served to jerk him from smiling down at Flora and standing idle like he meant to stay there the rest of the day. He swung into the saddle.

Flora took a step back, tipping her head to smile at him. A hairpin fell out and a wavy strand of hair escaped. She rolled her eyes. "Like Ma says, I have unruly hair. Pa says I have an unruly spirit."

He bent over to peer into her eyes. "Maybe you simply need to find where you belong."

Her eyes widened with surprise but before she could respond he rode away.

"Goodbye," she called.

He waved his hat in a salute then cantered out of town. The sun was warm on his shoulders and he slipped off his winter coat. The snow melted into puddles.

Spring was here. When a young man's fancy turns to love. He didn't know where he'd heard the words or if they'd sprung to his mind on their own, but it was true. He had two weeks to make Flora decide she wanted to marry him.

He returned home and tended the horse, filled the woodbox, and ate the last of the chocolate cake. He washed it down with coffee then looked about his house. It seemed larger than he recalled. Flora had only been there two days and yet he felt her absence like a huge piece of furniture had vanished from the room. Perhaps he should have gone along with the preacher's insistence that they marry. Or he could simply ride to the manse, sweep her up behind him on the horse, and claim her as his bride. He laughed at his foolish thoughts. Flora would laugh too.

He wandered around the perimeter of the room, paused at the window, and sighed. His gaze lit on the piece of wood from Pa's broken wagon then went to Esau's reins. For the first time in his life, he understood the restlessness that drove Esau and the determination that made Pa take a chance.

It was too nice to be indoors, so he strode out to the barn, saddled Blaze again, and rode out to check on his cows. They had sheltered near the trees as he'd hoped and now grazed contentedly on the bare patches of grass. Half a dozen spring calves followed their mothers.

Wouldn't Flora enjoy seeing this? Why not return to town tomorrow and ask her to accompany him?

He suspected she would be only too glad to, especially if she could wear her trousers and ride alongside him.

* * *

THE NEXT MORNING, he was ready to go to town right after breakfast but took his time getting there. He didn't want Flora to think he couldn't wait to see her. Or to make her feel crowded by his return.

He made a stop at the store before he went to the manse and knocked.

The preacher opened the door.

"I've come to take Flora for a ride."

"Nice to see you mean what you say."

Nice to know the preacher wasn't going to insist on an escort, though it seemed they might be past that need. "I want to show her my cows and the baby calves."

The preacher studied him.

Kade broached the next thing to conquer—how she would dress to accompany him. He knew the preacher's opinion, but he had his own. "I don't expect her to ride sidesaddle."

Dark eyebrows scuttled together and the man before him scowled. "She's a woman, not a boy."

Kade leaned back on his heels, grinning. "Pretty hard to make a mistake about that."

The preacher's scowl deepened but Kade pressed his point. "If I'm to become her husband, won't it be up to me to dictate how she can dress or ride?" He kept his voice low so none of those inside the house would hear.

Finally, the man relented and stepped aside. "Flora," he called down the hall. "You have a visitor."

Flora stepped from the kitchen, drying her hands on a towel. A smile crinkled the edges of her eyes.

"Didn't expect you back quite so soon."

"I thought you might want to ride out with me to see the cows and the newborn calves."

The blue of her eyes sparkled then the light died as she turned to her father. "Pa?"

The preacher sighed. "I already told him you have permission. Seems neither of you has a lick of sense."

Eve crowded to her sister's back and Josie and Victoria peeked around the door. Flora handed her towel to Eve. "I'm going riding." She grabbed a coat.

"I think you might want to change your clothes," Kade said, with a huge dose of amusement.

As she realized what he meant, a grin swathed her face. "It won't take me a minute." She clattered up the stairs and the door banged behind her.

Mrs. Kinsley came from the bedroom.

"How are the patients?" Kade asked.

Donny was hard on Mrs. Kinsley's heels and answered. "I okay."

Mrs. Kinsley patted his head. "You sure are. And to answer your question, Kade, Blossom is doing well. She's sleeping at the moment. It will take time for Stella to regain her strength."

Flora appeared in her trousers.

"Flora, I truly wish you wouldn't dress like that," Mrs. Kinsley scolded.

"It's all right, Ma. I'm going with Kade to see his cows. Pa said I could."

The parents exchanged a look then Mrs. Kinsley sighed. "Very well."

"Come on," Flora said to Kade.

He grinned at her impatience to be gone and they left the house. He caught his horse's reins and followed Flora around the house to the pasture behind the house and waited as she saddled Dollar. She chattered as she tacked her horse.

"My sisters were full of questions about what we did when I was stranded at your place. No one can believe you beat me at checkers." She stopped and looked at him over her horse. Her eyes were dark with emotion. Did losing at checkers affect her so deeply? But she quickly relieved him of that opinion.

"They were all so worried. Eve cried. She said she was afraid she'd lost the last of her family." She looked thoughtful a moment. "I am sorry they fretted." She mounted. "Lead on, Kade Thomas. Show me your cows."

Kade chuckled at her eagerness. "Follow me, Flora Kinsley." They grinned at each other, then he nudged his horse into a gallop and they raced out of town. Two miles later they slowed and walked their horses side by side.

She laughed for no apparent reason.

He gave her a look that silently demanded an explanation.

"It's far too nice a day to be stuck in the house baking," she said.

"Baking. Like more chocolate cake?"

"All kinds of cakes and pies and buns. Tomorrow is

Sunday, and we always plan for extra." She slid him a mischievous look. "You know, for all the lonesome cowboys who have started coming to church since we arrived."

He pretended to consider the idea. "It's for the preaching, I suppose."

"Oh, definitely. I doubt it has anything to do with Ma's food."

"Or the preacher's four daughters." They laughed together then fell into a companionable silence. After a bit he pointed out the landmarks. "You follow that little draw and there's a beautiful pasture with a little waterfall. Have you seen it?"

"Can't say as I have. Because, you know, as a proper young lady, I have never ridden out on my own to explore the area." She said it with convincing innocence.

For a moment, he thought she was serious then caught the flashing light in her eyes. It was his turn to laugh. "I wouldn't have thought otherwise."

She looked toward the draw. "One of these days…"

"I'll take you," he finished for her.

She turned, so he wasn't able to see her face and judge her reaction, but he guessed he'd see a touch of rebellion.

"The higher you go," he said, "the more chance of encountering wild animals."

She faced him but it wasn't fear he saw in her face, it was excitement. "Like what?"

"Bears, cougars, old trappers."

"All wild animals, huh?" She chuckled.

"Old trappers are the worst." He hoped she would take note of his warning.

She didn't respond and they rode onward until they

reached the river. They followed it toward the west and his cows.

"We're almost there." He angled away from the stream and over a little rise. His cows spread out before them. At this point they seemed content to stay together, close to home. As it warmed up more, he would need to ride herd on them to keep them from wandering too far. Unless he chose to let them run on the open range with the herds from the larger ranches. He hadn't decided. The latter meant he wouldn't need to herd them so closely. He simply had to take part in the fall roundup to claim the yearlings that were his.

The former meant he could put the bull of his choice with them.

She reined in beside him and studied the herd. "What do you have? About a hundred head?"

"You counted them?"

"Didn't you?"

"Yes, but they're mine. Why did you count them?"

"Curious, I guess. Looks to be twelve calves. All of them pretty sturdy looking."

He shifted in his saddle to study her more closely. "How do you know?"

She shrugged. "I told you. I'm good with animals."

"You said you trained your horse."

"Same thing." Her gaze scanned the cows. "Will you let them join the bigger herds on open range?"

"I might. Still haven't made up my mind."

To his surprise and delight, she talked about the pros and cons of letting them run with the bigger herds. "Advantages both ways," she said in conclusion. "I thought you might have some horses too."

"You sound disappointed."

"No reason I should be. Except I like horses. If I was a man, I'd have a hundred of them. But somehow I can't see Pa letting me do that."

She jerked upright, her eyes widened, and she pointed. "Look, a grizzly out of hibernation. It's the first time I've seen a grizzly. They are big animals."

"Yup. A person wouldn't want to run into one unexpectedly, especially if it was hungry. This one will be. I hope he doesn't have his mind set on beefsteak."

"Or us." They were downwind from the animal and sat motionless, holding their restless mounts as the bear ambled toward the river.

The cows bellowed for their calves and faced the beast. Kade knew they would protect their newborns, but it might cost them their lives.

The bear lifted his nose and *whoofed* but kept going.

Kade didn't relax until the bear was out of sight and, even then, he made the decision to return another way.

"Guess he's gone fishing," Flora said.

"I don't trust him not to come back and steal one of my calves. Do you mind if we stay and watch until I'm certain he's gone for the day?"

"Not in the least." They walked their horses toward the cows, keeping a goodly distance from the river and alert to the possibility the bear might return.

They crossed the pasture and climbed the hill on the other side then sat and watched the animals.

She glanced about. "This is a nice spot. Hey, look."

He followed the direction she pointed and saw the bear heading west, away from them.

"He might be moving up the mountains, but I'll be

keeping a close eye on my cows until I'm sure he's out of the area."

"Maybe I should come with you. Two pairs of eyes and two guns are better than one."

The idea of her accompanying him every day was mighty alluring. "I can imagine what your pa would say if he thought I was taking you out on bear patrol." He shuddered. "No thanks."

She chuckled. "He does tend to put the fear of God into people."

"I think you mean the fear of Preacher Kinsley." They grinned at each other.

The sun was at its zenith. "I suppose you're hungry," he said.

"You offering me fresh steak?"

He laughed. "Nope."

"You baked another chocolate cake?"

"Not yet."

She blew out her breath. "Then it's just idle chitchat you have to offer?"

"Maybe. Maybe not." He dismounted and lifted his saddlebags down. "Want to find out?"

"I am burning up with curiosity." She jumped down and joined him.

He flicked a strand of her hair and laughed. "Like Donny would say, you look like you are on fire."

She tossed her head as if it was of no matter. "Stop delaying and show me what you brought."

* * *

FLORA RESISTED the urge to reach for the lock of hair Kade had touched, but she wouldn't want him thinking it meant anything to her. Because it didn't. But his invitation for her to go riding with him seemed odd given Pa's anger at her having spent two days with Kade, and especially considering Kade thought her rash. And yet he had practically told her to wear trousers. None of it made sense. Did he miss her company? That hardly seemed possible after such a short time.

Was he trying to placate her pa? But she didn't see how asking her to ride with him accomplished that.

He opened the saddlebag and she pushed aside her questions as she leaned close to see what he had. He pulled out a slab of cheese and a loaf of bread.

"You baked bread?" She could not hide her surprise.

"You don't think I could?"

"I suppose you could. I just don't think you had time."

"I can't, but thanks for your confidence in me. Mrs. White had some freshly baked bread at the store, and I bought a loaf."

He pulled out a paper-wrapped package and opened it to reveal two fat dill pickles.

Flora's mouth began to water.

He sat on a grassy spot that the sun had dried and patted a spot beside him. "You hungry?"

"Sure am." She plunked down at his side and held out her hands.

"You can't have anything until I say grace."

"Yes, Father."

He tossed his hat to one side and bowed his head. "Thank you, God, for sunshine and snow and for adequate food for our bodies. Amen."

She grinned at him. "I like short and sweet. Maybe you could give Pa lessons on how to do that."

"I don't think so." He used his knife to cut a slab of bread for her and to slice the cheese in half.

She took one of the pickles and proceeded to build a thick sandwich. "You're afraid of my pa?"

"Are you suggesting I shouldn't be?"

"Oh, I would never do that." She leaned closer and lowered her voice. "Be afraid. Be very afraid." Their gazes caught and held, his brimmed with amusement. She was sure hers was too.

What was there about this man that she felt so comfortable with him that she could laugh and tease without concern for being judged? Especially given the fact he had been very outspoken about his disapproval of her? Did he still feel that way? She longed to ask but was afraid of what his answer might be.

She wrapped the bread around the pickle and tried to take a bite. It was too thick and she had to settle for nibbling at it. "Yum. Delicious. Thanks for thinking about food."

"Sorry it's not cake."

"A person could get tired of sweets all day long." She longed to add, just as a person might grow tired of someone who never took any risks. But although she would have liked to hear it on her behalf, she understood that he had suffered too many losses to ever get to that point. "I suspect a person could." She left it at that.

They sat side by side, enjoying the simple lunch and watching the cows. The calves lay down together with one cow guarding them while the others moved on, seeking any shoots of green grass.

After a bit, he got to his feet and held out a hand to pull her up. She came face to face with him, only inches between them, close enough for her to see that the irises of his brown eyes had a black circle at the edges. Close enough she could see the dark stubble on his cheeks. Without thinking she lifted her hand and rubbed his chin. "Bristly," she said.

He caught her hand and held it to his chest. "It's called whiskers."

Was his voice husky, or was it only rumbling past a bump in her brain?

He cleared his throat and stepped back, releasing her hand. "It's time to get you home."

She avoided looking at him as they mounted up and rode away, avoiding the river and the possibility of encountering a bear.

What had she been thinking, to be so bold as to touch his face?

CHAPTER 11

ade wakened the next day with an eagerness that was foreign to him. He jumped from bed and ate the rest of the loaf of bread and a huge bowl of oatmeal porridge he had left cooking throughout the night.

The sky had blushed pink when he jogged to the barn to saddle Blaze. He let the animal warm up then galloped over the hills to where his cows grazed. He puffed out his lips with relief when he saw they were all safe. Just the same, he wouldn't be able to relax until he was certain that grizzly bear posed no danger. He skirted the herd and made his way to the river, following the tracks as they went west, alert to any sign the bear had returned. An hour later, he was satisfied. For now. He galloped back to his house. He didn't bother to unsaddle his horse. He'd left water heating. He put six inches into a square wash tub, shed his work clothes, and bathed.

He pulled on clean clothes and studied himself in the mirror. He slicked his hair back, thinking he might have to go to town and get it cut. He grinned. Sure didn't mind an excuse to venture into town on a weekday. He'd have to come up with a whole bunch of excuses in order to court Flora without her growing suspicious.

He glanced at the clock. He'd have to hurry to get to town before the church service started. Half an hour later, he reached the church. People filed in. Several cowboys hitched their horses, hung their hats on the saddle horn, ran their hands over their hair, then headed for the door.

Kade did the same. He walked inside the church and waited for his eyes to adjust to the muted interior. As he expected, the Kinsley family were already seated in the front row. He marched up the aisle, excused himself past Victoria and Eve. Flora watched him approach. If he wasn't mistaken—and he was almost certain he wasn't— she looked pleased and perhaps a little surprised when he sat down beside her. He hoped that in the next two weeks he could persuade her to be pleased every time she saw him.

"Hi," he said.

"You've come to hear the preaching, just like all the others." She glanced past him to the assembled cowboys.

"Yup. I'm here for the sermon."

They grinned at each other then faced forward before her ma could scold them for whispering in church.

Kade wasn't much of a singer but he sure did enjoy listening to the Kinsley girls. Josie played the piano. Most of the hymns were unfamiliar to him, seeing as he had so seldom been inside a church, but he liked the words of some of them.

Then preacher Kinsley opened his Bible. Before he

began, he fixed a hard look at Kade. It was all Kade could do not to squirm, but he would not blink before the man. Kade respected him, but he had to make sure Flora's pa understood that Kade would not be intimidated.

The preacher shifted his gaze to include the entire congregation. "Today I am going to speak about God's love."

Whoa! Kade had expected a fire and brimstone sermon, a be-sure-your-sins-will-find-you-out lesson. Directed to Flora as much as anyone. Maybe the man wasn't as hard as he let people believe.

The preacher's voice softened. "Too often we mere mortals take God's place and judge our fellow man. Yes, God is a righteous judge, but He is not without mercy and love."

By the time the sermon ended, Kade felt as if heaven had opened and poured love down from God. He longed to ask the preacher how he could deliver a sermon like that and yet justify the way he dealt with Flora. Not that Kade was any different. He suddenly realized that he'd been treating Flora just like her pa did. He was concerned Flora's rebel ways would lead her into a dangerous situation from which there was no escape. If Eagle Pete had spent the storm with her, rather than Kade, things would have turned out much differently. He shuddered to think of it.

"You'll join us for dinner?" Mrs. Kinsley said as they stood to leave.

"Thank you, yes."

She extended the invitation to half a dozen others as she made her way down the aisle.

Kade nudged Flora. "Maybe they came for the meal invite."

She grinned. "Ma knows how to get people to attend church."

"Cowboys at any rate." He suspected some of them had never stepped into a church until they heard of the preacher's unwed daughters.

A man he didn't know scowled at Kade as he exited with Flora at his side. Kade tucked a grin into his heart. Seems there were others who might have their eyes on the rebel redhead.

They crossed the yard to the manse, skirting puddles left from the melting snow.

Inside, the house was a hive of activity as the visitors were welcomed and the daughters helped put out food.

Mrs. Kinsley pointed out where each one should sit, and it ended up there was a cowboy on either side of each Kinsley girl. Blossom, who still looked pale, sat next to Mrs. Kinsley. Donny at her other side.

Kade asked after Mrs. Norwood, who had not made an appearance. He assumed she was resting.

"She is improving," Flora's mother said. "It will take some time for her strength to return."

The preacher stood to ask the blessing. Kade discovered the man was thankful for a lot of things and not opposed to praying for the souls of those gathered round the table.

Flora nudged him as if to remind him how she liked his short graces. He clamped his teeth tight as amusement filled him. He knew if he chuckled aloud the preacher would be offended and likely take him to task.

"Amen." The preacher sat down.

The cowboy across from Kade blinked several times. Kade wondered if he had dozed off during the grace. Again, he stifled a chuckle.

Then there was a flurry of passing the platters and bowls around. Mrs. Kinsley and her daughters had prepared quite a feast—roast chicken, mashed potatoes, gravy, carrots, turnips, and buns that were impossibly light. He knew Flora would have learned to make food like this and the idea of coming home to a hot meal every day made him want to take her home as his wife this very day.

Mrs. Kinsley gently guided the conversation. She asked each visitor to tell a little about themselves. Two of the cowboys were hardly able to speak beyond giving their names. Turned out they were brothers who both rode for one of the big ranches to the west. Kade guessed they spent most of their time in silence, surrounded by cows and cowboys who had little to say.

Then it was Kade's turn, and he felt every member of the Kinsley family studying him. He knew they were assessing him as a mate for Flora and sought for answers that would make them see him as suitable.

"Do you have family elsewhere?" Mrs. Kinsley asked.

"No family." He explained that his parents and brother were dead. He provided only the barest of details but glanced to Flora as he said his brother and father had died in separate accidents. Her soft expression made the telling less painful.

They wanted to know where he'd come from and what he'd done until he started ranching, and he provided the answers.

Two of the other cowboys scuffed their feet under the

table as if annoyed that Kade took up so much of the Kinsley's attention.

The conversation turned to community events as Josie and Victoria removed the food and the plates. Flora and Eve brought forward three beautiful cakes and two pies.

"There's chocolate, white, and spice cake, and apple pie," Mrs. Kinsley said. "Have your choice or two or three."

Without waiting for him to say what he wanted, Flora sliced into the chocolate cake, slid a piece onto a dessert plate, and handed it to Kade. Their eyes connected and in that moment, they shared a sweet memory.

And he felt a world of possibility in life shared with this woman. At the end of two weeks, they would be married according to her Pa's orders. Kade would enjoy the benefits of having a woman in his house. But he wanted her there of her own accord, not reluctantly and resentful. He had thirteen days to make her want to marry him.

As soon as the meal was over, Kade turned to Flora at his side. "Would you care to walk with me as soon as the kitchen is cleaned up?" He knew from his previous invitations that the Kinsley girls were expected to restrict Sunday activities to visiting, sedate walks, or playing the piano and singing—all of which were enjoyable enough, but Kade wanted to be alone with Flora. He'd like to tell her how much he had enjoyed the sermon and ask her how she saw God. And perhaps, just enjoy her keen sense of humor.

"Why, yes, that would be lovely." Her words and

demeanor were sweet and demure but her eyes flashed as if she was as eager as he to be alone.

"Can I go too?" Donny asked.

"Of course, you may," Mrs. Kinsley said.

"Me too?" Blossom asked.

"No dear. You need to rest."

The little girl's lips quivered then she yawned. Already her eyelids drooped. The Kinsley girls chuckled.

A short time later, Kade and Flora headed for the door. Donny trotted after them. The others rose and headed down the hall. For a moment, Kade feared all the sisters and cowboys would follow them, but they turned aside to the parlor and one of the girls began to play the piano.

They skirted the puddles in the street as they made their way toward the heart of town. The buildings were new and proud. Many of the businesses on Main Street boasted a false front as if to convince everyone they were bigger than they truly were.

They wandered down the street toward the edge of town where the Buck River meandered by. They made their way to it. Someone had thoughtfully placed a wooden bench nearby and they sat there. Donny tossed stones into the water.

"Your pa surprised me with his sermon," Kade said. "All about God's love."

"Don't you believe He is a loving God?"

"Guess I never thought of it much."

"I think of it a lot. Seems to me God is more loving and merciful than most people."

He considered her words a moment. "You find it easy to trust Him?"

They studied each other. Perhaps she, as did he, realized they were exploring each other's values at a deeper level than they had done so to this point.

"It's easy to trust someone you know loves you."

He felt a world of warning and possibility in her words.

She continued. "And yet, I feel as if there is something in here—" She rubbed at her breastbone. "Something missing. Or perhaps something I've forgotten. I try and find it. Sometimes I try and escape the feeling."

He caught her restless hands and covered them with his. "I hope you find what you are looking for. I hope you find peace."

She didn't argue or deny she needed to find peace. Nor could he explain how he knew that's what she needed. Except he did.

After a moment of searching his gaze, she nodded. "That would be nice."

They sat in companionable silence, their hands clasped together.

Then she spoke. "Do you find it difficult to trust God? I mean with all your losses, it must be hard." She turned her palm to his and squeezed.

"I suppose I am a bit like you. I don't hold God responsible for what a man or woman decides to do. But I realize there is more to believing in God than that. It's like you said when you saw the Bible in my house. It needs to have a place of honor in my heart. Guess what I mean is, I need to give both the Bible and God a bigger place in my life."

"I like that. I want to do the same."

"Seems we are agreed on that matter." He felt a

surprising jolt of pleasure at having reached common ground on their beliefs.

"It's not the only thing we agree on." She sounded hurt.

"What else is there?" He meant to be teasing, but he wanted to know.

"We agree that chocolate cake is good. That eating it for breakfast doesn't matter. That riding is fun and grizzly bears are dangerous."

He chuckled and squeezed her hand. "And maybe that Eagle Pete is just about as dangerous?"

"And that little boys tossing stones are fun to watch?"

"That too." He could add a few more things. That sharing a bench by the river on a sunny Sunday was about as nice as one could dream.

Donny grew tired and joined them on the bench. The boy had recently been sick. They needed to get him home, so they meandered back, none of them in a hurry to reach the manse.

Kade's horse was the only one remaining at the rail, which meant the other cowboys had left.

"Guess I should be on my way."

"You're welcome to stay for supper," Flora said.

"Thanks." It was tempting and he was pleased she invited him but... "I think your family might be wanting a bit of peace and quiet."

"It's not like you're noisy."

He grinned. "Are you saying you'll miss me?"

She shook her head. "I'm only thinking of you having nothing but chocolate cake to eat."

"It's all gone." He sighed deeply. "Guess I'm back to potatoes and eggs. I bought some more eggs from Mrs.

Ellis, you know." The woman lived on the edge of town, which made it easy to pick up eggs as he rode to and fro.

"No, I didn't know. But if you're happy eating that"— she waved her hand in the air as if he deserved what he chose—"then by all means, go on home."

"I think it's best if I do." He didn't know who it was best for, and the lonely half-hour ride back held no appeal. But it was home. The place where he felt safe. Where he hadn't let unnecessary risks intrude.

Until now.

Was he risking his future happiness by courting this woman?

Not that he had a choice in the matter. Her father had made that clear.

* * *

THAT NIGHT FLORA knelt on one side of her bed, Eve on the other, as they silently said their prayers. Flora finished first as always and crawled under the covers. Eve followed shortly afterwards and put out the lamp. They lay side by side. Flora's thoughts were on the afternoon spent in Kade's company.

"You're smiling," Eve said.

"How can you tell? It's dark."

"You were smiling when I got into bed. You still are, aren't you?"

Flora's smile widened. "Maybe."

"You like him, don't you?"

Flora pretended she didn't know who her sister meant. "Who?"

"Kade. You like him."

"I like talking to him. It doesn't mean anything."

"Do you like him well enough to marry him?"

Flora turned to look at Eve's gray outline. "I saw you talking to that cowboy. What's his name? Oh right. Claude. Does that mean you like him well enough to marry him?"

"I was only being polite. Besides, I didn't spend two days and two nights alone with him."

"Would it have been better to perish in the storm?"

Eve squeezed her arm. "Of course not. I'm glad you were safe. But like Pa said, not everyone will be so understanding."

Flora admitted to herself that the two days had been almost enjoyable. She might have even grown to like Kade's company a little bit.

Which did not mean she had to marry him. Or wanted to.

But Pa had said she wouldn't have to. Hadn't he? She tried to remember his exact words but could only recall how relieved she was that he had said the wedding was off.

CHAPTER 12

*T*he next day Flora donned a faded blue dress that was roomy and comfortable, ignoring Eve's *tsk* of disapproval. Eve had threatened to throw it into the ragbag on more than one occasion, but she held her tongue. Flora was grateful she did so. She was in no mood to argue about what she wore.

They descended to the kitchen. Ma shook her head at the worn dress but said nothing.

Flora almost sniffed. They should all be relieved she didn't wear her trousers. And maybe they were, which would explain why they did nothing more than reveal their disapproval with looks.

It was Monday and as such, it meant doing laundry. Flora enjoyed hanging the garments and then removing them when they were dry, so that was her share of the work.

It provided her plenty of opportunity to study the landscape as she pinned damp clothes on the line, laughing as they blew around her body. Time and again, she stood with her hands on the line and the clothes billowing around her. Ma called to her twice that she was falling behind.

She quickly finished the task and as she returned to the house, glanced down the road leading south. Not that she expected Kade to visit, but if he did, he would come from that direction.

"Would you see to Stella?" Ma called. "Take her tea and toast."

"Yes, Ma." She quickly prepared the snack and carried it into the bedroom.

"How are you feeling?" She plumped pillows behind Stella so she could sit up.

"Much better. Your ma tells me to expect it to take a few days for me to get my strength back."

Flora knew her ma had said a few weeks, but she didn't point it out.

"Where are my children?"

"Donny is digging a hole in the dirt. Says he's looking for buried treasure. Blossom's sitting in the sun with a rag doll Ma found for her. She's where we can keep an eye on her."

"You people are so good to me. It makes me feel guilty."

Flora patted Stella's arm. "It's what we do. We help people."

"Well, it's very good of you, and I am beholding."

"No need to feel that way. All of us owe something to someone, and sometimes the only way to repay it is to help another person."

"That's a very kind way of looking at things. But I can't believe you owe anything."

"My parents died when I was younger than Donny. The Kinsley's took in both me and Eve and adopted us."

"I didn't realize." Stella grew thoughtful. "It must have been hard losing your parents. If it happened to my children—" She choked off and couldn't go on.

"Being a Kinsley is all I remember." She looked past the walls of the room into her past. "Except for what Eve has told me about our parents. Our pa died when I was a baby and Eve only two. She was six when our ma passed, so she remembers more."

"I'd say you are a fortunate young woman."

"And I would agree." She rose, preparing to leave.

"Please don't go. I feel so alone here."

So, Flora sat at her bedside and told her about the Kinsley sisters. "All adopted." And their older brother. "He's not adopted, but we haven't heard from him in almost two years."

"How dreadful." Stella grew pale.

"I must let you rest." Flora took away the tray and tucked the covers around Stella.

As she left the room, she thought of what she owed Kade. First, for sheltering her through the storm and then for persuading Pa not to force them to marry. She would make it up to him somehow. One thing she could do was save him a portion of the chocolate cake. If he came.

She stared out the window. What made her think he would come? He had work to do. So did she. She turned away from staring down the road.

Maybe he would come in the evening. She made sure some chocolate cake remained, and if anyone wondered at her hoarding it, they didn't say anything.

But he didn't come that evening.

She wasn't disappointed. Why would she be?

* * *

THE NEXT MORNING, she ate the last piece of cake at breakfast.

"Flora!" Ma was satisfyingly shocked.

Josie laughed. Victoria gave one of her gentle smiles, and Eve shook her head in exasperation.

"Nothing in the Bible against it," Flora said with a touch of defiance.

Pa banged his fist on the tabletop, making the dishes and the females jump. "You will show your ma respect."

"Yes, Pa." Though she was at a loss to understand how eating a cake for breakfast constituted disrespect.

"Where is that young man of yours?"

He must mean Kade, but hers? Why would he say that? "I'm sure I don't know, Pa." She kept her head down, afraid what else Pa might have to say.

Instead, he harrumphed and took the Bible for the morning reading.

It was Tuesday, which meant there was ironing and mending to do. Flora took the mending and sat in the sun on the front porch. Donny and Blossom played nearby.

Eve came out with a basin of potatoes to peel. "Flora, you're staring into space."

She was actually staring southward, but she let Eve think her mind wandered. "Do you remember our real father?"

"No. He died when I was two."

"I don't remember what he died from."

Eve grew thoughtful. "I don't remember either."

"But it wasn't doing something foolish, was it?"

Eve studied her a moment before answering. "As far as I recall, he was ill. But what an odd question. Why would you ask that?"

"Just thinking." Kade lost his loved ones to risky choices. She'd lost hers to other reasons. Her mother had been ill. Somehow it all seemed connected. Or was she trying to look for connections that weren't there?

She set aside the basket of mending and hurried out to the stable, ignoring Eve's questioning call.

Her trousers were in the house, so she saddled her horse, tucked her skirts around her legs, and rode away, galloping until her hairpins fell out and her hair blew free.

She reined in on a hill that overlooked the town. Why did she have this incredible urge at times to ride away? Was Kade right? Was she trying to outrun something? That didn't make sense, but she couldn't think what else it might be.

Maybe she was searching for something. But what? She had a good, loving home. She had kind sisters. Her brother, Josh, was gone. She missed him, but it didn't make sense to think she could find him by riding hard.

Besides, this urge had surfaced long before Josh left.

Why this restlessness?

She turned Dollar to the south. Without having made a decision to do so, she rode toward Kade's place. Talking to him seemed to help ease her restlessness.

Half an hour later, she reached his house and called his name. When she received no answer, she opened the door. The house was empty. So was the barn and the outbuildings. She rode toward the cows. They still grazed contentedly in the sheltered pasture. But Kade wasn't there.

What did she expect? That he would hang around waiting for her to drop in?

Her gaze went to the trees where the grizzly had gone. What if he'd encountered the bear? Her heart jolted. Maybe he lay somewhere, injured, bleeding—horrible images filled her mind. There was only one way to calm her fears.

Slowly, cautiously, she made her way around the herd toward the river, pausing often to strain for any sound that would indicate the nearby presence of a bear or a man moaning in pain.

She reached the river and leaned over Dollar's neck to study the tracks. Not that she was good at it. She saw a paw print that was wider than her hand. Then she made out a set of tracks from a horse. But she didn't know what it meant. She had no way of judging if the bear sign was new or from Saturday.

Or if the horse was Kade riding up the river or someone else.

A tremor raced across her shoulders and she carefully studied her surroundings. Was the bear watching her from nearby or even some man? Had the sheriff let Eagle Pete out of jail?

She reined about, made her way through the trees, then galloped toward home. She slowed the pace once she could see the town. By the time she reached the yard, Dollar had cooled off.

Ma watched her approach and shook her head.

Flora tended her horse, rearranged her skirts, and braided her hair. Knowing what to expect with her wild hair, she'd taken to keeping a store of ties in the stable. She selected one to secure the braid.

Ma stood in the doorway to the house, waiting for her.

"Ma, I'm sorry I am such a disappointment to you."

Ma gave her a hug. "Child, it isn't that I'm disappointed. I'm worried. Since the day you came to us, you have had this urge to run. I thought you'd outgrown it, but lately it's back, worse than ever. Child, what makes you want to run away?"

"Oh, Ma, I'm not running away. I love you. I love my family. But there are times I feel like I have to escape or I'll burst at the seams."

"Flora, all I can do is pray you will find your peace."

"Thanks, Ma." Kade had said something similar. How odd that they both seemed to know what she needed when she didn't. She could perhaps understand Ma being able to see Flora more clearly than she saw herself. But Kade? It didn't make sense. She barely knew him.

He barely knew her.

* * *

FLORA FLUNG from her bed Wednesday morning and rushed downstairs without putting her hair up.

Ma and Pa looked up at her hurried entrance into the kitchen.

"What's for breakfast?" she asked. "What do you need me to do?"

Ma handed her a bowl of thin porridge. "Take this to Stella and make sure she eats it all."

"It looks like baby food."

"Her stomach is still weak. Send the children out and I'll feed them."

Flora's sisters descended and the kitchen was soon a flurry of activity. Flora hurried to take care of Stella.

She prowled the room as Stella ate.

"You're restless today," Stella said.

"I get like this sometimes."

"Why? What's bothering you?"

Flora plunked down on the chair by the bed. "I don't know." This restlessness was different than what she'd felt yesterday. She had no urge to ride away. In fact, she didn't want to leave.

"Maybe you're missing Kade." Stella's words fell into Flora's brain like they meant to stay.

She considered them a moment. "Maybe."

"He's a nice-looking young man."

Flora chuckled. "I'll tell him you said so. If I see him again."

"Don't you tell him." Stella's cheeks flared with color. "And you'll see him again. Mark my words."

Flora tipped her head to study Stella. "How can you say that with such assurance?"

"Because I've seen how he looks at you."

"With dismay."

"No. The two of you worked like one when you found me and the children."

"That was because it was a crisis."

"No. It was because you fit together."

Flora pushed to her feet. "Are you done?"

"Yes, thank you. If I've offended you, I'm sorry."

Flora stilled her urgency to leave. "I'm not offended, but I don't see it as you do."

Stella's smile seemed to contain a world of wisdom. "That's all right."

Flora joined the others for breakfast, then helped do the morning chores, which she could probably do in her sleep they were so familiar. Ma announced it was time to prepare the garden for spring planting.

"Can I do it?" Flora asked. She much preferred being outdoors. And hard work would be an antidote to her restlessness.

"I thought you'd like to."

A little later, Flora straightened from digging the soil. It smelled fresh and promising. She'd finish before dinner, and the family would work together in the afternoon to plant the seeds. Donny dug in the dirt at one end of the garden. The boy sure did like digging.

Her gaze searched the road going south. Would he come?

Why should she think he might? Why should she care if he did or didn't? She jabbed the shovel into the ground and turned over another scoop of dirt.

Donny stood up. "Someone coming."

A rider approached from the south. It was Kade. It was all Flora could do not to run out and meet him on the road.

* * *

Kade saw Flora standing in the garden. Strands of her hair fell around her shoulders, catching the sunshine. Like Donny said, her hair looked like it was on fire.

He skirted the church and rode directly to her.

She watched him, shading her eyes with her hand and making it impossible for him to see what she was thinking. Was she glad to see him? Or had she been relieved not to have him around? The clock was ticking on her father's decree to persuade her to want to marry him. Ten days left.

He jumped to the ground and stood at the edge of the garden. "Hi." He knew he sounded tentative, and he was.

"Where have you been?"

He grinned. "You missed me."

"I worried about you." She jabbed the shovel into the dirt. "I rode out there yesterday. Your house was empty. I checked your herd. The cows looked fine." She turned over the soil. He glanced past her and saw the entire garden except for this last corner had been worked.

She continued, her words sharp. "Then I got to thinking about that grizzly and rode to the river to make sure it hadn't circled back and attacked you." She jabbed the shovel into the ground with a force that made him wince.

"It's nice to know you care."

Another stab of the shovel. "Who says I care?"

He laughed. "Let's see. You ride out to see me, and when I'm not there you begin to worry about me. Yup, you care."

She leaned the shovel against the fence and crossed to plant herself toe to toe with him. "Where were you?"

He caught her hand. "Walk with me and I'll tell you."

He preferred to have her alone without the curious study of a little boy and the interest of her sisters as they crowded to the window to watch.

She looked toward the house, then nodded. "A walk is a good idea."

The town ended at the back of the yard and they strode toward the river. The warm sun had dried up the last of the late spring storm. Green grass tinted the ground.

They came upon the river a distance from where they'd sat on the bench Sunday and instead sat on the grassy slope, watching the water ripple past.

"You want to know where I was the last two days?"

"I guess."

He laughed, finding pleasure in the way she pretended she wasn't almost overcome with curiosity. He decided to tease her a little. "Well, if you aren't interested…" He waited. How long before she would demand he say?

She sighed. "Fine. Tell me."

"You sure?"

She faced him. "Kade, just tell me, okay?"

"Fine. I will." He caught a strand of her hair and tugged it gently. "Monday morning I decided I had to make sure the grizzly was not going to return and help himself to one of my calves, so I started tracking him."

She shuddered. "It's pretty risky tracking a hungry bear."

He shifted his hand from her hair to her shoulder. "I was careful. I don't take unnecessary risks."

Their gazes caught and held. She searched deep. He let her, searching equally deep. They had begun this conversation when she ended up in his house during the storm. He had said similar words then, but they felt different now. Had talking to her, listening to her views on risks, understanding a little about why she ran, changed him? Had being with him changed her at all?

"Good to know." Her voice seemed deeper than usual. "What did you find?" She meant his tracking.

"I followed the tracks for a distance, then the bear left the river and veered to the south. I kept following, thinking he was hungry and circling back to the easy pickings of spring calves." His hand still rested on her shoulder. She might have pressed into his hand or he might have imagined it.

"The bear meandered about. I could see where he unearthed a den of some smaller animal. Might have been a rabbit." A patch of blood indicated the bear had managed to capture something to eat. "I saw where he'd nosed through some berry bushes hoping to find something. He went into a stand of trees." Flora shivered.

Kade enjoyed a moment of knowing she feared for his safety. "I rode around the edges looking for tracks to indicate the bear had left the trees. I found them and continued to follow the trail." He paused, still dismayed from what he'd found.

"I came upon a homesteader. The bear had been there."

Flora gasped.

"It wasn't as bad as it might have been. The farmer had a milk cow. The bear must have threatened her or simply frightened her. She'd panicked and ran into the wire fence. Somehow, she'd gotten tangled in it. And of course, the more she struggled, the worse it got." It was distressing to see her torn and bleeding." I helped to free her, but it took quite a bit of time. We doctored up her wounds. By then it was almost dark, so I accepted the invitation to spend the night with the man and his little family. He has a wife and two young sons."

"Good idea. That was Monday."

He heard what she didn't say. Where was he Tuesday? He grinned. "I know you missed me."

She looked at the river, avoiding his gaze.

He chuckled. "Wouldn't hurt to admit it." Then he continued his story.

"The next morning, I started tracking the bear again. Midafternoon, I saw him in the distance. He was on the ground, not moving. The farmer had said he shot at the bear but didn't think he hit it. I wondered if he was mistaken. I rode a bit closer. I didn't want to alert the bear to my presence, especially if it was wounded and cranky. Then I saw the bear had a carcass. He'd found something to eat. I don't think he'll be back."

"Sure hope not."

He finished the story. "I made my way home after that. Stopped to check on the farmer. He was worried about his cow, so I had a look. I think she was mostly still agitated, but I helped him clean her wounds again and put on salve. Then I rode home." It was late in the day by the time he arrived and although he was weary, he still considered riding to town to spend some time with Flora. Instead, he'd decided to head for town first thing the next morning.

"And now here I am."

She grinned at him. "If I'd known you were coming, I would have baked a chocolate cake."

It was on the tip of his tongue to say he'd be there every day in the hopes of making her agreeable to marrying him, but if he said that, she would resist his courting.

In the distance, someone called, "Dinner."

"I think that's for us." Flora held out her hand to invite him to accompany her.

He did so, anticipating a good meal and the hope of the rest of the day in her company.

Preacher Kinsley greeted him with a look that seemed to say it was about time he showed up and got serious about his courting.

Throughout the meal the girls amused him with their teasing and their questions.

He helped do the dishes afterwards though the girls all protested. Flora grinned at them. "He's mighty handy in the kitchen."

A beat of silence, heavy and surprised, greeted her remark, and then the girls all began to talk at once.

He tried to think why they had reacted that way then realized it was because she referred to the two days they'd spent together unchaperoned. Even her own sisters found it startling. He couldn't imagine what those outside the family would think.

Except he could. He must work harder at winning her over to the idea of marriage.

He went to the parlor to speak to her pa. "I'd like to take Flora riding this afternoon."

"In trousers?"

He didn't answer, because the man knew the answer and simply had to express his displeasure.

The preacher waved him away as if to say, *she'll soon be your problem.*

Kade was getting used to the idea. Indeed, he didn't find it the trial he might have not very long ago.

He returned to the kitchen. "Do you want to go with me to check on my cows?" he asked her.

Her eyes lit. "Can I change?"

He nodded and she raced up the stairs. He faced Eve.

"I hope you know what you're doing," she said.

"I believe I do."

Eve studied him a long moment. "She's my little sister, and I would not want anything to happen to her."

"It won't."

Flora clattered down the stairs, grabbed his hand and, laughing, half dragged him out the door. She saddled her horse and swung to his back, where she sat grinning at him.

"I don't know how you persuaded Pa to let me do this."

He'd assumed she knew why he was spending so much time with her although, at the same time, he hoped she didn't. Knowing would make her resistant.

But not knowing made his secret seem underhanded.

What would happen if she learned the truth?

CHAPTER 13

Over the next few days as Flora spent time with Kade, she wondered over and over why Pa wasn't objecting to her riding with Kade or Ma didn't complain that she was neglecting her share of the chores. But she wasn't going to ask for an explanation and perhaps bring an end to her enjoyment.

On Friday, Kade said, "Would you like to go see the falls tomorrow?"

She fairly jumped at the idea. "Yes."

"Let's make a day of it."

"I'll bring a picnic." She grinned at him, barely able to contain her excitement. "I thought you would forget your offer to take me."

"Sure didn't."

She patted his shoulder. "Good thing. What time shall we go?"

"I'll leave home as soon as it's light."

As soon as he left, she rushed inside. "I'm going to

make a picnic for us tomorrow," she announced, not caring who heard her.

"Can I come?" Donny asked.

"It will be too long a day for you."

Ma looked about to protest when she heard about Flora planning a long day, but a glance from Pa and Ma lifted her hands in resignation.

Flora looked from one to the other. Had they decided they no longer cared what she did? Was she somehow not worthy of their concern after being stranded with Kade?

And then Eve asked, "Where are you going?"

"To a waterfall." She opened the cupboards. "What will I take? Ma, can I have this leftover chicken?"

"Go ahead. There isn't enough to make a meal from it."

Eve and Flora looked at each other and grinned. Ma could turn almost anything into a meal. Soup at the least.

"I'll make a cake." She pulled out the bowl and pan and soon had a chocolate cake in the oven. Should she make sandwiches or more of a dinner?

She recalled the simple lunch they'd shared a few days ago—why that would be almost a week ago.

Simple seemed to suit them so she made sandwiches, wrapped two dill pickles, and as soon as the cake was baked and cooled, iced it. Everything was ready for tomorrow. Now all she had to do was wait...something she'd never been good at.

She could hardly sit through supper and forced herself to appear calm. But when she went to bed, she wondered if she had succeeded.

"You're sure excited," Eve whispered as they lay side by side in the dark.

"I can't wait to see the waterfalls. I wonder what they're called."

From the bed across the room, Josie laughed. "Are you sure it's just because you're going to see the waterfalls?"

"I'd love to see them," Victoria said.

"Maybe Flora would take you along." Josie made it sound like Flora was waiting for someone to suggest it.

"We're going on horseback." Flora managed to keep her voice regretful.

Her three sisters laughed.

"What? I know Victoria doesn't want to spend the day riding a horse."

Eve patted Flora's hand where it lay on the covers between them. "We are all quite convinced that is the only reason you don't invite her along. Or any of us."

She heard the teasing note in her sister's voice but tried to pretend she didn't. "You can all come if you like." She knew she sounded peeved and her mood wasn't improved when the girls laughed at her invitation.

"No thanks," Eve said. And the others agreed.

Flora flipped over on her side determined to ignore their teasing. She had never been up close to a waterfall and the idea thrilled her. Did she like the idea of going with Kade? She admitted she did. He no longer criticized her or made judgmental remarks about her behavior. More than that, he had suggested she wear trousers for riding and Pa hadn't objected. Nor had Ma. It didn't make sense, but she wasn't going to mention it and perhaps remind them of their oversight.

* * *

SHE WAS out of bed the next morning before the sky showed any sign of sunrise.

Eve groaned. "Go back to sleep. It's still dark out."

"I've got things to do."

"Then go do them."

"I will." She tiptoed down the stairs and past Ma and Pa's room. She paused outside Stella's room, listening for any sound that indicated she needed something. All was quiet. She left the house through the back door, pausing to put on her riding boots. They had once belonged to Josh but thanks to Ma's edict that nothing was thrown out—"It might someday be useful"—Flora had a good pair of boots.

Her insides dancing with anticipation, she pressed back the hurrah rising in her throat, went to the pasture, and softly called, "Dollar."

He trotted to her and let her rub his head.

The sky went from black to grey to pink. The small, scattered clouds glowed golden. It was going to be a good day.

A few minutes later, she heard Ma and Pa in the kitchen and then Josie said something. The household was up. Flora went inside, quickly set the table, then stopped at the stove to judge how long before breakfast.

"Pour the coffee." Ma indicated the bubbling pot and Flora carried it to the table. Pa always got the first cup and then Ma. After that, she made her way around the table, filling four cups for herself and her sisters. Stella still rested in bed, too weak to join them.

She sat. The others followed her example. Pa's prayer was far too long. She much preferred Kade's short ones.

It took time to eat and then Pa brought the Bible to the table to read the daily portion. Flora couldn't have said what he read. As soon as he closed the Bible she jumped up, gathered the dishes, and took them to the dishpan, washing them with a haste that meant three sisters had to dry to keep up. As soon as she finished, she grabbed the lunch she'd prepared and dashed outside. Kade would be here any minute and she didn't intend to keep him waiting. She sat astride her horse when he rode up.

"I see you're ready. Been waiting long?"

"Nope. Perfect timing."

His eyes flashed with teasing. She guessed he was about to ask if she missed him, but she didn't give him a chance. She nudged Dollar and raced from the yard.

With a shout, he followed her.

She bent low over Dollar's neck and urged him to greater speed. Glancing over her shoulder, she saw that Kade did the same. They raced for two miles and then he caught her. Of course, she might have let him do so. She looked at him and laughed. The sort of laugh that had built with each stride of her horse...that had been held in too long. Perhaps long before this day. She reined in, tipped her head back, and let the sound pour from her, coming from deep inside. Bringing in its wake a joy that filled her to such an extent that she couldn't stop smiling.

He smiled, too, though perhaps with a bit of puzzlement.

"That was fun, wasn't it?" It didn't begin to explain how she felt. She wasn't sure she could, but as they rode onward, she tried. "I don't know when I've felt so free." She waved her arms in the air to illustrate her point. "I've never before had anyone who would ride with me like that. Even Josh always made me stay back, as if I was a hindrance to him."

Kade continued to cast puzzled looks her way. "You often feel like people are holding you back?"

She sobered. "I've never thought of it that way, but maybe I do." Shifting so she could study his face, she asked, "How did you figure that out when no one else could? Ma just says I have always wanted to run."

Their horses had stopped moving as Kade and Flora studied each other, their gazes locked. She couldn't say what he sought. For that matter, she couldn't say what she looked for. Only that she hoped she would find it. She shook her head at her foolishness and turned away from looking at him.

"Are we going to the waterfall or not?"

"I haven't changed my mind," he said with a degree of amusement.

"Nor have I." Side by side they rode up and down the hills until they reached the place he had pointed out to her earlier. Hills rose to the right and the left. Rocky crags poked out from the dirt. The valley narrowed as they climbed. The incline grew steeper.

Kade paused and turned, indicating she should look behind them.

She gasped at the view. The land fell away from where they sat. "I can see for miles. Is that Buck River?" A darker green line indicated the trees that stood along the river.

"Yes. Amazing isn't it?"

She drank in the view, filling her lungs with the fresh air. "It smells green."

He chuckled. "Green is a color, not a scent, but I know what you mean. The air is full of new growth and the promise of good things to come." He shifted in his saddle to grin at her.

Again, their eyes caught and held as if something fragile hung between them and any sudden movement would shatter it into a thousand pieces.

His smile faded, his eyes darkened.

She got the feeling he searched deep into her thoughts, perhaps even went so far as to touch her soul. She'd never before experienced anything like it and couldn't explain what it meant except it made her jittery. At the same time, an incredible calm edged into her very being.

With a gentle smile he reined his horse around. "Let's go see that waterfall."

They rode up and up. And then he paused. "Do you hear it?"

She stopped and listened. "A trickling sound. No, a hum."

"A hum. I like that. Come on. We're almost there."

The path they followed was rocky and uneven. In a few minutes they dismounted and left the horses. Kade held out his hand and helped her over the rugged ground. They passed between two boulders and then before them lay the falls. A series of four steps and then a drop-off. He guided her to a rock bench and they sat. Silent and mesmerized.

The falls weren't overly loud. The gray sheets of water were interlaced with silvery threads. Water dripped from the nearby rocks. Birds sang with abandon.

Flora couldn't look away.

Kade nudged her. "What do you think?"

Her throat was too tight for her to be able to answer. She reached for his hand to grip it.

He chuckled. "I kind of thought you would feel that way." He put an arm about her shoulders and squeezed her to him.

She rested against his side, content to be enjoying the moment without thinking of anything beyond this place of solitude. "It's so peaceful," she murmured after a bit.

He didn't say anything, simply tightened his arm about her.

Flora might have sat there forever except her bottom was getting sore from perching on the hard rock. She pushed to her feet.

Kade stood too, and they looked into each other's eyes. His dark and full of emotion. There was no need for words between them as they shared something deep and meaningful stemming from this place.

"I brought a picnic," she murmured. "It's in the saddlebag."

They scrambled over the damp rocks, between the two boulders, and returned to the horses, where she took out the lunch. Her gaze went to the path they had followed to the falls.

"Do you want to eat where you can see the water?" he asked.

She nodded.

This time he led her on a different route, and they found a grassy spot where they sat with their backs to a rock. She opened up the sack holding the food and handed him a sandwich.

They ate in companionable silence.

"I have never experienced anything like this," she said, hardly able to tear her gaze away from the falls. "It's peaceful and yet so powerful. It echoes here." She pressed her palm to her chest.

"Peace yet power. I like that." He shifted to look into her face. "Amazing to think that we can enjoy both in our lives."

She met his gaze. "What do you mean?"

He turned to study the waterfall for a moment then edged closer to her. "I remember the first sermon I heard your pa preach. He read a verse from the Bible about God's yoke being easy, His burden light. At the time I wondered how that was possible. A burden is a burden. A yoke is a yoke. I don't recall his exact words, but your pa said two things make them easy. The fact that God loves us and frees us from our sin. And that Jesus walks beside us so every burden is easy, every yoke light. It's the same with peace and power. Or peace and freedom."

She considered his words. Seems he and Ma were always advising her to seek peace. Could she have peace and freedom? Peace and—

Her thoughts stalled there. As always, she couldn't say what it was she wanted. But rather than try and sort it out, she returned her attention to the falls. Maybe someday she would find the answer to her questions. Maybe someday she would know what the question was. But she didn't want to ruin the peace she had found here.

"Oh. I have chocolate cake." She had put the cake in a

bowl and wrapped it tightly in brown paper to keep it from falling apart. She'd brought a fork just in case.

One fork? What was she thinking?

She uncovered the bowl to discover something that looked more like dry pudding than chocolate cake. "It was a nice slab of cake when I left home."

Kade looked in the bowl and sniffed. "It smells good. I expect it will taste just as good."

"I have one fork." She held it up.

He took it from her before she could think. "Thanks." He scooped up a forkful of cake and popped it in his mouth. "Good."

She giggled. "You stole it." She reached for the fork, but he was prepared and held it out of her reach. "Oh no, you don't." She was on her feet instantly. So was he and held the fork out to her.

"Here, your turn."

But when she went to take it, he again held it out of her reach, laughing at her failure.

She stopped. Her arms fell to her sides and she stared at him. "I've done this before."

"I know. Back at my house during the storm." He waved the fork in front of her. "You'd think you'd know by now that I'm too fast for you."

"It wasn't you." Tears leaked from her eyes, trailed down her cheeks and a sob erupted from the depths of her heart.

* * *

HE SHOULDN'T HAVE TEASED her. She didn't like this game. Kade offered her the fork. "Here. Take it. I'm sorry for teasing you."

She shook her head. "It's not about the fork or the spoon," she choked out.

"I don't understand."

Sobs shook her. Tears streamed down her face. Her distress sliced his heart into a dozen bleeding pieces. He pulled her into his arms and pressed her face to his chest.

"Flora, what's wrong?"

She sobbed so hard she couldn't speak so he held her, wishing he knew what was the matter and how to fix it.

"I shouldn't have teased you."

She shook her head.

"Then what?"

Again, a shake of her head and a gut-wrenching sob.

He pressed his cheek to her head and closed his eyes, feeling her pain in corners of his heart that had been locked up since the deaths of his father and brother. Maybe closing his heart had started before that with the many goodbyes to his mother.

He held her tight. Sorrow this deep was a stinging thing.

Finally, she quieted. Her arms slipped about his waist. "Hold me. Just hold me."

He was only too glad to do so. He widened his stance as she leaned into him.

"It wasn't about you teasing me." Her voice was thick from crying. "Remember I said it seemed I had done it before?"

"I remember."

"Well, I did. It was with my big brother. He would

play a sort of game with me where he put something on the table, and we would reach for it to see who could get it first. He always did, but it made me giggle."

"A fun game. Josh seems to have played a big role in your life."

"It wasn't Josh. Eve said we had a brother. Timmy. He was a lot older than us, though I don't remember exactly how much. I always thought I didn't remember him. Eve used to get so angry with me and want to know how I could forget him. She said he took care of us after Papa died." The words had a jagged feel to them, as if carrying shards of pain.

"Maybe it hurt too much to remember him."

She jerked, pushed back, and stared up into his face. "Yes, that's it."

He smiled down at her, glad he could help her see what it meant.

She held his gaze as she continued. "He was gone. I realize now he went to get help for Mama, who was so sick. But we waited and waited for him. I remember how worried I got. I had to find him and tell him how afraid I was and then he would come home and tell me it was all right. So, I ran out the door. I ran as far as the gate but then Eve caught me and dragged me back. She said we had to stay and wait. But I was desperate to find him. I remember how badly I wanted to leave. I thought if I ran hard enough, fast enough, I would catch him. I was four. Little did I know how impossible it would have been."

"What happened to him?"

"He died. The neighbors found him. I think he was thrown from his horse, though I can't really remember. I'll have to ask Eve."

"Did she never tell you?" Kade couldn't imagine why Eve would keep it a secret.

"I didn't want to talk about it. Every time she mentioned Timmy, I shut my mind to her voice. Or I'd block my ears. Or run away. If she insisted on telling me, I would cry. So, she quit.

"He made me feel safe. And then he was gone. And I didn't know if I would ever be safe again. Which is silly, because what could be safer than being adopted by the preacher and his wife?"

"Not losing those you love."

"I guess you understand, having lost people you love."

Tears had made tracks down her cheeks and dried. Kade rubbed at the trails with his thumb.

Her eyes widened. Her lips parted.

He studied her mouth. Slowly, giving her lots of time to let him know she didn't want the same thing he did, he lowered his head and caught her mouth with his. He tasted the salty brine of the recent tears. He heard the sudden intake of her breath. Her arms tightened around him.

He'd only meant to offer her comfort, but awareness and longing filled him, surprising him with its depth. He had to force himself to withdraw for fear of frightening her.

But he was in no hurry to leave this place. He pulled her back to the grassy spot where they'd been sitting. Their backs rested against a boulder. He kept his arm about her, smiling as she leaned into him.

Would now be a good time to formally ask her to marry him?

CHAPTER 14

*K*ade had kissed her. And she'd liked it. But what did it mean? Surely it meant he was growing fond of her. Did she welcome that?

She grinned. It would be nice so long as he wasn't set on making her reform.

He had drawn her down to the ground and kept his arm around her. She clung to him. Remembering Timmy had broken down a barrier she'd created in her mind. "I was always afraid to remember him," she murmured. "I think I feared the pain."

"I can understand that. How do you feel now?"

She considered the question. "It hurts. I suppose I will always miss him. Perhaps that's why I clung so doggedly to Josh. I didn't tell you, but I cried buckets when he left." She gave a chuckle. "I made sure to do it in private." She shifted so she could look into his face. "That's why I've always felt the need to run, isn't it?"

He smiled, his eyes dark and full of kindness.

She rested against his chest and studied the waterfall. "What's the name of this place?"

"I haven't told you. How neglectful of me."

She heard the teasing in his voice and playfully jabbed him in the ribs. "Yes, it is."

"Ow." He captured her hand and she made no effort to free it. "It's called the Cascades."

"A pretty name for a pretty waterfall."

A cascade of memories flooded her mind. "I remember Timmy chasing me and tossing me in the air when he caught me. He read to us before he tucked us into bed. I suppose that was only after Mama fell ill."

"I'm glad your memories have returned."

"Me too. I can understand why I shut them away when I was young, but I should have allowed them back long before this."

"It sounds to me like they were locked up and you needed something to unlock the door."

"Guess that was you." She felt him stiffen as if surprised by her observation. "How does it make you feel to know you did this for me?"

"I'm happy for you."

She heard a reservation in his answer and sat up to look into his face. "You don't sound convinced." His eyes were dark and searching.

"I just realized I have locked doors inside me as well."

She waited for him to continue, sensing that he needed time to find the words. Perhaps even to discover what to do with those locked doors. She knew when he'd reached that point as his eyes softened and smile lines creased out from their edges.

"I have been so afraid of being disappointed by people's actions and hurt by more death that I closed myself off to caring about anyone again."

"And that's changed?"

He grinned. "I believe it has."

"Good. I'm glad to hear it." She brushed her finger across his lips. Her heart broke into a gallop at the way he smiled.

He caught her hand and pulled her closer, looking deep into her eyes. "I think we are good for each other."

She waited, unsure of what he meant.

"Maybe we shouldn't have been so quick to say we wouldn't marry."

Stunned, she sat back and stared at him. "Have you changed your mind about marriage?"

"I've always wanted a family of my own."

He'd said that before.

"There's really only one reason to marry, and that's because you can't imagine life without the other person."

They considered each other as the waterfall rumbled on without pause.

She waited a moment, but when he didn't say anything one way or the other, she sat back against the rock, a cold inch between them, and turned her gaze to the cascading water, trying to regain the sense of peace she'd had a short time ago.

"Peace and freedom. Is it possible?" she asked.

"Love is a risky business."

"Maybe." She understood that love could lead to loss and pain. Why was she even thinking about love? It wasn't that she wanted him to love her.

"I don't think it can be rushed." He jumped to his feet and pulled her up to follow him as he drew closer to the water. "But maybe it can be encouraged," he murmured in her ear. Not giving her a chance to reply, he turned her toward the mist. "Let's just enjoy the waterfall." He stood behind her, his arms around her shoulders, leaning back so she automatically leaned into him.

She closed her eyes and let the comfort of his arms, the solidness of his body, and the murmur of the water drive away everything but this moment.

All else faded and they were as one, wrapped in the beauty of their surroundings.

Which might, she readily admitted, include being held in his arms.

She couldn't say how long they remained thus. Time stopped until he slowly lowered his arms, catching her hand. She shivered at the loss of his body warmth.

"It's cooling off."

At his words, she realized he had protected her from the falling temperatures. She glanced upward. A few clouds. Surely nothing to be concerned about.

He saw her study of the sky. "The sun is dipping into the west. It cools off quickly up here."

Flora looked about. Dark shadows clung to the boulders and climbed up the surrounding hills.

"We need to go." Still holding her hand, Kade led her back to the horses. He didn't immediately release her.

She looked into his face and, at the gentle smile upon his lips, she leaned forward. She couldn't say if she invited a kiss or wanted the comfort of his arms or if she only wanted to prolong their stay here. "It's been a special outing," she murmured.

"It sure has." He caught her shoulders and pulled her close, tipped her chin up to study her, his gaze searching her eyes, down her cheeks, and stopping at her mouth.

"Very special," he whispered before he kissed her.

She clung to him, breathing in the dampness still clinging to him, her heart unfolding like the petals on a spring flower newly emerged from the ground.

He chuckled as if reading her thoughts. "Like I said, we need to go."

They took the reins of their horses and made their way down the rocky slope until they reached less treacherous ground, then mounted and rode down the draw.

Down the hill, the air was still warm with the sun. There seemed no need to hurry home, so they took their time. Their conversation consisted of talking about the countryside, the growth of the town, and Kade's hopes for a growing herd.

They passed the church and rode to the stable. Kade dismounted and waited as she tended her horse. Done, she spoke to him. "Would you like to join us for supper?"

He glanced at the sky. "I think I'll ride home before dark."

She hoped she hid her disappointment. But perhaps she hadn't succeeded, for he caught her chin and waited for her to meet his gaze.

"I think that was one of my best days ever."

"Me too."

He rode away, pausing before he passed the church to wave goodbye.

She returned the gesture and stood watching until he rode from sight, then realized she smiled so broadly that if anyone saw her, they would wonder what made her so happy.

And what could she say? If this wasn't love, it was close enough to satisfy her.

* * *

KADE HADN'T SAID he would return for church on Sunday, but Flora hoped he would. She wore her blue dress and worked hard to get her hair into a neat roll.

"Do you want help?" Eve asked after Flora failed three times to put in enough pins to keep it in place.

"Yes, please." Flora sat on a stool with her back to Eve and let her sister tackle the wayward curls. The other girls had already gone down. Victoria was playing the piano at church this morning and was likely already over there.

"You seem very pleased with yourself today," Eve said.

Flora realized she was smiling. "I am. You know how I could never remember Timmy? Well, yesterday I did." She told Eve all the things she recalled.

Eve knelt at Flora's knees. "It always surprised me that you insisted you didn't remember him. All this time you did, but the memories were locked up. What happened to free them?"

Flora wasn't sure how much she wanted to tell her sister, but it seemed safe to say it had been because of a silly tease about sharing a fork. "I remember Timmy playing a similar game with me." As she talked, she realized it was more than the game. It was Kade himself. His frankness with her. His steadiness. How safe he made her feel.

Would he have arrived at church yet? Her legs twitched with the need to rush over and see. She patted her hair. "Are you done?"

"Just about." Eve put in more pins. "There you go."

Flora bolted to her feet.

"Wait for me," Eve said, checking her own reflection in the mirror.

Flora forced herself to keep a sedate pace as they walked down the stairs, out the front door. She glanced at the horses tied to the rail. When she saw the black horse with the white blaze across its forehead, her pace quickened so much that Eve protested and she slowed.

They stepped inside. Kade waited at the doorway. "May I escort you two fine ladies to your pew?" It was Flora he looked at and Flora's hand he pressed hard to his side as she took his arm.

Eve chuckled.

Flora was grateful the light inside the church was muted as her cheeks burned. Not with embarrassment as others might think, but with pleasure at knowing he had waited for her.

They went three abreast down the aisle although it meant her skirts caught on the pews as they passed. They slid in beside Josie and sat down.

Flora forced her gaze to Pa and did her best to listen to the sermon knowing he often asked the girls questions about it. But the words went in and out of her brain so fast she couldn't recall a single thing.

The service ended. Ma invited several cowboys to join them for dinner.

Flora helped serve the meal and listened as the new cowboys introduced themselves, but she knew if she later met them on the street, she would not remember them or their names.

The meal ended, the dishes were washed, and they all made their way to the parlor. Flora had hoped Kade would suggest they go for a walk, but he seemed set on listening to the music.

Flora told herself she wasn't disappointed. Why should she be?

When the others rose and said goodbye, he got to his feet as well.

She was about to think she had imagined the events of the previous day.

"Walk me to my horse?" he said.

Finally, he was showing her a bit of attention. "Of course." They crossed the yard to the rail. The others left one after the other until only Flora and Kade stood there.

"What are you doing tomorrow?" he asked.

"It's Monday so we'll be doing laundry."

"Oh." Did he sound disappointed?

"You're welcome to come help."

He laughed. "I have to take care of a few things and check on the cows but maybe I'll ride in later in the day."

"Okay."

"That is, if I'm welcome."

She drew back. "Why wouldn't you be welcome?"

He twisted his hat in his hands. "Well, I got to thinking I might have offended you by kissing you."

"So that's why you've been acting so distant." The hat was taking a real beating.

She leaned close, grabbed his shirt lapels, and pulled him toward her. She planted a quick kiss on his mouth. "Does that seem like I'm offended?"

"Nope." He grinned widely. "Sure don't." He swung into his saddle and raced from the yard. Before he was out of sight, she heard a *whoop*. She forced herself to stop grinning as she returned to the house.

CHAPTER 15

*K*ade whooped several times on the way home, making his horse a little skittish. He threw together a meal of bacon and potatoes. "Sure would be nice to have someone cook me a meal once in a while." Someone with fiery red hair and a spirit to match might be the perfect person to do it for him.

Maybe it was time for him to ask the gal to marry him. Before the next five days and the preacher's deadline. The preacher had warned him today that he meant to proceed Friday, whether Kade had made any progress or not in persuading Flora to welcome the idea.

Kade didn't want the forced marriage. He wanted Flora to marry him because she wanted to.

Because she couldn't imagine living without him?

Well, he had no objection to that, but it wasn't entirely necessary. Being ready and willing to work together would be enough.

He tried to plan how to ask her, but he didn't know how it was done. Did he just blurt it out? Did he take her someplace special? The only place that came to mind was the waterfalls, and he didn't want to wait until they had time to go there again. Nor could he afford to. The preacher wouldn't be lenient about how long he'd wait to see his daughter married and her reputation intact.

* * *

HE WOKE the next morning with no more idea of how to propose to Flora then he had when he went to bed. He was tempted to ride to town as soon as he had breakfast and simply blurt it out, but she'd said they would be busy doing laundry, and he had chores to take care of. He cleaned the barn then wandered around the place. Watching Flora work on the garden had made him think he might plant one himself. He looked for a suitable spot.

Perhaps he'd work on it another time. For now, he wanted to check on the herd. He saddled his horse and rode that direction. He counted them and found he was three cows short. Alarm skidded through his veins. Had the grizzly returned? He should have checked them before instead of entertaining Flora. Was he getting as careless as his pa or brother?

But as he rode toward the river, he knew it wasn't carelessness that controlled him. It was a desire to spend time with a woman who made him laugh and enjoy life.

Not wanting to surprise a bear with its food, he approached the trees with caution. He soon discovered why the cows were missing. Each of them had found a place in which to have their calf. They snorted a protest when he approached but he managed to guide them back to the others where there would be a degree of safety.

A glance at the sun, and he knew it was close to noon. Was it possible to reach town in time to get dinner? It was worth a try.

He kept up a steady pace until he got to the manse and left his horse in the pasture behind the house. Laundry flapped on the line.

No one appeared at the door or window. Had they not heard him? As he approached the house, he heard singing and smiled. He knocked. The singing ended and Josie opened the door.

"Hi, Kade. Come on in. Flora's been hoping you'd come."

"Josie!" Flora protested.

Kade chuckled as he hung his hat by the door and stepped inside. The meal was obviously over. He'd have to go without food.

"Have you eaten?" Mrs. Kinsley asked.

"No, but I'm fine."

"Nonsense. Flora fix him a plate."

"Yes, Ma." She filled one to overflowing and set it before him. "I wasn't waiting for you," she murmured close to his ear. "But that doesn't mean I'm not happy to see you."

He grinned at her. "Thanks." Let her wonder if he meant for the food or for her admission.

As he ate, he glanced about the room.

Josie peeled vegetables. Victoria chopped something into a bowl of flour. Eve cleaned the stove. The preacher sat at the end of the table, reading his Bible. He gave Kade a look so full of warning that Kade almost choked on his mouthful. And then his gaze slid by the man to the woman in a rocking chair watching the activity.

"It's nice to see you up, Mrs. Norwood," Kade said.

"Thank you, and please, call me Stella."

Blossom whined at her mother's knees. Donny jostled her out of the way and the little girl cried.

Stella closed her eyes, obviously too weary to cope with her children's demands.

Mrs. Kinsley looked around the room and saw that Flora appeared to have nothing to do but watch Kade eat. "Flora, kindly take the children outside and amuse them."

"Sure, Ma." Flora tilted her head to indicate she wanted Kade to accompany her. She lifted Blossom.

"Come on, Donny." They headed out the back door.

Kade cleaned his plate, took it to the cupboard. "Thanks for dinner." He followed Flora outside.

Blossom fussed. "Let me take her." He didn't know if he could soothe her or not, but it was worth a try.

Flora shifted the girl into Kade's arms.

Startled, Blossom stopped crying and looked at him. Then she opened her mouth and wailed. He turned her so she couldn't see him, made comforting sounds, and walked back and forth. She stopped crying then slumped in his arms.

"She's fallen asleep," Flora whispered. "Let's sit."

She pointed toward a row of chairs against the house.

He lowered himself to the wooden seat of one, careful not to disturb Blossom. He adjusted her so she looked more comfortable. He lifted his head to meet Flora's gentle smile.

"What?" he whispered.

"You like children?"

"I like the ones I've met."

Her smile widened. "It would appear they like you

too." Donny sat beside Kade's chair playing with a carved dog.

Kade smiled. He'd always wanted a family. A place to belong. A place of warmth and welcome.

He sat back. It was on the tip of his tongue to say to Flora, "Marry me." But even though he wasn't sure how to ask her, he knew this wasn't the way.

He held Blossom as she slept. Sometime later, the little girl wakened with a cry, scrambled down, and ran inside. By then the laundry was dry and Flora went to gather it.

Kade watched her reach for the line, bend as she put the folded item into a basket, and then do it again, the laundry flapping about her torso. She sang a hymn as she worked.

The basket full, she carried it to the house.

"You seem to enjoy this task," he said.

"I do. I love the smell of clean laundry." As if to prove her point, she leaned over the basket and sniffed. "Don't you?" She held the basket in front of him and he dutifully sniffed.

"It's nice. I never noticed before." Wouldn't she be shocked to know that his clothes were often washed in the river, sometimes still on him? On occasion he took a stack of things to a woman in town and paid her to do his laundry.

"I'll be right back." She hurried inside and returned in a few minutes to take the rest of the laundry from the line. She paused at his side. "You coming in?"

He followed her indoors. They were already setting out supper. Where had the afternoon gone?

He was invited to stay and did so, but he wanted to be

home before dark, so he prepared to leave shortly afterwards. He asked Flora to walk him out.

Her father stood by the garden. Was he watching them? Or seeking solitude to think? Whatever it was, with the man nearby, Kade had no intention of asking Flora to marry him, and most certainly not of seeking another kiss.

"Flora, I want to go check on the homesteader tomorrow. It worries me some to think the grizzly might return to his place."

"I understand." She lowered her voice. "I might even miss you."

He chuckled as he rode away.

* * *

MIGHT MISS HIM?

The next day, Flora missed him with an ache that hurt from the top of her head to the bottoms of her feet. She had to keep busy to keep from dwelling on the loneliness sucking at the marrow of her bones, but after she'd burned the clothes twice with the iron, Ma chased her away from that task.

By noon the ache was so intense Flora could barely eat. As soon as the meal was over, she raced from the house, saddled Dollar, and galloped away.

Without giving it any thought, she rode south. As soon as she understood she was going to Kade's place, her insides calmed, and she settled into an easy pace. She knew exactly what she would do.

She would prepare him a proper meal that would welcome him home.

He'd shown her his cold room, and she chose a selection of vegetables. He had canned jars of meat he purchased at the store. She made biscuits, stew, and chocolate cake. Maybe next time, she'd get a jar of apple filling from Ma and bake him a pie.

Everything ready, she took a chair outside and sat, her chair tipped against the wall of the house. From her position, she looked toward the west where the homesteader lived.

She waited, smiling in anticipation of how pleased he'd be. She continued to wait. Hadn't it been sweet to watch him with Blossom? He'd make a good father. The sun dipped toward the mountains.

She knew she must leave if she wanted to get back before dark.

Accepting that her plans were not to be achieved, she returned the chair to the house and removed one place setting from the table. At least he would enjoy a meal whenever he got home.

It was almost dark by the time she reached town.

Ma waited for her at the door. "Flora, where were you? I was getting worried."

"Sorry, Ma. I didn't mean to cause you any problem."

Ma made a scolding noise. "I kept a plate for you."

"Thanks." She wasn't hungry, but to refuse would make Ma worry even more so she sat down and ate every bit of the food set before her.

"Where is everyone?" The house was very quiet.

"Your father is at the church, studying or praying."

Likely praying for his wayward daughter, Flora thought.

Ma continued. "Stella and the children are asleep.

Victoria went to bed with a headache. Eve and Josie went for a walk. They should be back soon. It's almost dark." The door opened and the pair stepped in.

"It's a beautiful evening," Josie said. "We saw a deer and a new fawn at the river."

Eve looked at Flora. "When did you get back?"

"A bit ago." It was stretching the truth, but she had no desire to get involved in one of Eve's scoldings.

She washed her plate and put it away. "I'm going to bed."

When the others came up, she pretended to be asleep.

* * *

The next morning, Flora wakened feeling like the bed had become a prison. No one else was awake as she dressed and tiptoed from the room. Everything was quiet downstairs, but a light shone under the crack of the door to her parents' room. She eased down the hall, hoping she could pass the doorway without alerting them to her presence.

She heard Ma say her name and froze. "Flora is not getting ready for her wedding, and it concerns me."

Wedding? Wasn't that over? She pressed to the wall, unable to move until she heard what Ma meant.

"You gave Kade two weeks to court Flora and convince her she wants to marry him rather than force her unwillingly into a marriage. The two weeks are almost up and there's been no change. But her reputation has been compromised. They will have to marry whether they want it or not."

Her father's deeper voice answered. "I thought he had

a good idea—win Flora over so she wouldn't enter into a marriage she didn't want. You know how stubborn she can be. How she holds an idea forever."

Ma made a sound of agreement.

Pa continued. "They are spending a lot of time together and seem to enjoy each other's company. He has three more days."

Flora didn't hear what else was said. Kade had been courting her simply to convince her it was what she wanted? All the time and attention he'd been showering on her was so he wouldn't have to deal with a wife who resented being forced to marry him?

And here she'd been thinking how much she liked him. She'd even thought he liked her.

It was all pretend.

She tiptoed down the rest of the hall and across the kitchen floor, paused outside the door to pull on her boots, and then ran to the pasture. Minutes later she was on Dollar's back galloping northward.

The sky flared pink, mocking her pain.

No matter how she felt, she would never misuse her horse. She slowed to consider what she meant to do.

There was only one place she wanted to be. She turned Dollar that direction.

* * *

KADE ENJOYED another serving of stew and chocolate cake for breakfast, smiling all the while he ate. Flora had come out and made him supper. There was only one thing wrong with it. She wasn't there to share the meal.

Soon that would change. They would marry and she would be there every day.

He ignored the way his thoughts knotted at the idea of her being forced to marry. But then, no one was forcing him. A laugh unexpectedly burst forth. How did the preacher intend to force them? Somehow, he couldn't see the man threatening to shoot either of them. Or either of them being convinced he'd do it.

He washed the dishes he'd used. Having her prepare his meal was the nicest surprise he could ever remember. He couldn't wait until she saw the surprise he had for her.

He had decided how he would ask her to marry him. Had reasoned that afternoon was the best time to ask her. The sun would be warm that time of day.

He'd even found a patch of yellow buffalo beans that were ready to blossom, and they might be ready by then.

While he waited, he took care of chores and made a quick trip out to check on his cows. He ate the last of the stew and cake, and then rode to town. He paused as he reached Glory, studying the church, the house, and the yard. Everything appeared peaceful. He didn't see Dollar, but the horse might be on the other side of the stable.

What if she wasn't there? It was one thing he hadn't taken into consideration.

Only one way to find out. He tied his horse in front of the house and knocked.

The door flew open. "Thank goodness, you're here," Eve said. "Is she with you?" She looked past him.

"Who?" Alarm skittered along his nerves. He looked about the room. Everyone was there but the red-headed gal. "Where is she?" And why was everyone looking so concerned?

Everyone talked at once, making it impossible for him to understand.

"Girls, stop." The preacher's firm words put an instant end to the chatter. "Mother, give the man a cup of coffee." Mrs. Kinsley hurried to obey her husband. "Kade, sit down."

Kade perched on the edge of a chair. Mrs. Kinsley put a cup before him and Kade wrapped his hands around it. "Has something happened to Flora?"

The preacher held up his hand to signal quiet as the girls clustered about wanting to talk. "She was gone when we got up this morning and she hasn't returned."

"Gone? Where? When?"

"We thought she might be with you."

Kade shook his head. "But doesn't she often ride off? Why is this any different?"

"Because when she returned yesterday, she wasn't her usual self."

Eve spoke. "She went to bed early and pretended to be asleep when we followed her up. It isn't like her. I'm concerned."

Kade tried to make sense of this. "She's out riding, that's all." There was nothing unusual about that though he was disappointed she wasn't there.

Mrs. Kinsley sat across from Kade. "Eve says she's remembered her brother and bits of her past. That concerns me. When she first came to us, she wanted only to run away. It didn't matter to her that she didn't have a destination. I knew she wanted to find her brother, Timmy. But that wasn't possible. She's never gotten over that urge to run. I fear she has given into it." Flora's ma's voice shook with emotion and she pressed her hand to Kade's. "I assume she was with you yesterday. Perhaps you know what's going on with her."

"I didn't see her yesterday, but she was at my house." He explained how he'd been away, and she'd prepared him a meal. "I don't see that as being a reason to upset her." Were these people being overly concerned? Flora was known for riding off and being gone long hours. "She must have been out there most of the afternoon." He hoped pointing it out would make them understand this wasn't any different.

"It was almost dark when she got back," her ma admitted. "I can't explain how I know it, but this is different." She sent a desperate look at her husband. "I must tell him everything."

The preacher nodded and Mrs. Kinsley turned back to Kade. "I think she might have overheard a conversation between me and her father. I thought I heard the floor outside our room creak and then a minute later the door rattled as it does when anyone goes in or out." She went on to explain how she'd asked her husband about Kade and Flora. "I knew he had given you two weeks to persuade her to marry you of her own free will."

Kade's insides crackled. "Did you say that?"

The woman nodded. "I mentioned that you were courting her for that express purpose."

Kade groaned. "I don't think she'd take kindly to that information."

"She certainly wouldn't. I feel so guilty." Mrs. Kinsley squeezed his hands. "Would you please find her for us?"

He was already on his feet and headed for the door before she finished.

Now Flora would have reason to doubt everything Kade had planned to say.

He automatically headed south, out of town. But he'd not seen her near his place. Where would she go?

One place came to mind. He prayed she would be there and be safe. At least Eagle Pete was behind bars. Of course, that wasn't the only danger she might encounter. There were bears, wild cats, wild men...

He couldn't think about it.

He galloped toward the waterfall.

If anything happened to her...

He couldn't imagine life without her.

He slowed when he reached rocky ground. Her horse was tied at a tree. He left his horse, to slip and claw his way higher.

Knowing it unwise to rush into any situation, he slowed, strained to hear anything above his own ragged breathing. The only other sound was the tumbling water.

He eased forward, not wanting to alert anyone who might have come upon Flora. And then he saw her and stopped.

She sat on a rock, her knees drawn up, her chin resting on the backs of her hands.

He studied her profile, trying to gauge her feelings.

She shifted and saw him. "Go away. I don't want to talk to you."

"Your family is worried about you."

"I'm fine."

He edged closer. "Your ma thought you might have overheard something she said."

Flora stared at the water. "I hoped I would find peace here again."

Kade reached the rock and leaned against it, his head level with her feet. "Nothing here has changed."

"I have." She shifted. For a moment, he wondered if she meant to kick him. "How could you?"

"How could I what?" He tried to sound confused but wondered if he succeeded.

"Pretend to want to spend time with me. Pretend to have fun with me. Do things with me."

"I wasn't pretending."

"You told Pa you'd court me and persuade me to want to marry you." She jumped from the rock and went to the edge of the stream.

He followed. "I wasn't pretending."

She refused to look at him. "This place made me think I could have peace and freedom."

"You can have more." He let the words settle between them then added, "You can have love and freedom."

She shot him a disbelieving look. "By being forced to marry you? Seems to me I would have neither." She moved to her left, widening the distance between them.

"Flora, think about it. Do you really believe your father could force us to get married? How would he do that? Threaten to shoot us?"

The way she looked at him convinced him she had not considered this.

"If I marry you it will be because I want to." He spoke softly, calmly.

"If?"

"I plan to marry you, if you're agreeable."

"Why?"

There was only one right answer, and he could honestly provide it. "Because I can't imagine life without you."

She stared. Opened her mouth and closed it again. Then shook her head and turned away.

"You're just saying that."

"No, I'm not, and I think I can prove it to you." He hoped she'd be convinced by what he had in mind.

"I don't see how." She remained stiff and acted disinterested.

"Come back to my place and see for yourself."

She stared at the cascading water as she considered his request.

Finally, she nodded. "I warn you, it's going to be hard to convince me."

He laughed, as much from relief as amusement. "Trust me. I know."

* * *

FLORA KEPT a healthy distance between herself and Kade as they returned to the horses. It was curiosity that made her agree to accompany him. Nothing more. Certainly not any hope that he could prove what he said.

I can't imagine life without you. He only knew what to say because he'd heard her mention it a time or two.

She must build a solid wall around her heart before they reached his place. Otherwise she would break down and say how much it had hurt to learn his reason for courting her. Why had she allowed herself to think he cared? To believe that her heart was safe with him?

He pointed out a few things as they rode. The purple,

frosted-looking crocuses. The hawk above them, a mere pinprick of black. The new green leaves on the Thimble-berry bushes.

She took it all in without answering, afraid if she opened her mouth, she'd say far more than she wanted to.

They approached his house. It had taken some time but not long enough for her insides to settle into steel.

"Thank you for the meal yesterday. I'm sorry I missed you, but I surely did enjoy the food."

"You're welcome." To her relief the words had come out solid and firm.

"I wouldn't mind coming home to a hot meal every day." He let the words hang in the air a moment as if he expected her to have something to say.

When she didn't offer anything, he sighed. "And a warm welcome."

Oh, if only he knew how badly she wanted to offer that to him. But in return, she ached to feel safe and loved.

He rode toward the barn and she followed.

He dismounted. She did the same. He opened the gate to the pen and indicated she should follow him into the little pasture. *What are you doing?* She could barely keep her curiosity silent.

She heard a whinny. Strange that it sounded like it came from in front of them when the horses were behind.

Then Kade stepped aside. A beautiful chestnut filly with a flaxen mane and tail watched them curiously, nickering a greeting.

Flora could no longer keep silent. "She's a beauty."

Kade stepped closer to the filly. "Come and say hello."

Flora could not refuse. She petted the animal. "She's the prettiest horse I've ever seen."

"She's yours."

"What?"

"I had it all figured out how to do this. I was going to invite you to go riding with me and then bring you here and as I asked you to marry me, I would give you the filly."

"Why?"

"As a wedding present, I guess." He shrugged. "It seemed like a good idea at the time."

"No, I mean why were you going to ask me to marry you when Pa was going to make you do it?"

"I have no intention of marrying someone against my will or theirs. There is only one reason to get married and that's because you can't imagine life without the other person. Flora, I need you. I want you." He looked so desperate she almost relented, but she wanted to be sure of her decision.

"I love you," he said. "I want to see you every morning, every night. Every minute of the day."

"I'm a wild rebel. You said so yourself."

"Flora, you can ride as much as you want. You can wear trousers if you like. You can herd cows or train horses. I'm offering you love and freedom. Please say you'll marry me."

He offered her everything she could ask for and even more than she had dreamed of. Love, freedom but more importantly, an understanding heart. Her own heart opened like a blossom welcoming warm sunshine. "How can I say no? You've promised me everything I've ever dreamed of." Hope brightened his eyes.

"Kade, I can't imagine life without you." She closed the distance between them. "I love you."

He opened his arms and she willingly, eagerly, went to him. She lifted her head for a kiss.

He caught her lips with his and kissed her long enough, firmly enough, that she was almost satisfied. But her hungry heart wanted to be kissed again.

After a bit she shifted to rest her head on his shoulder. "Kade, my heart has found a resting place."

"Flora." His voice was deep. "I know my heart is safe with you."

EPILOGUE

Most of the congregation had left when Flora took Kade's hand. They left the pew to stand in front of her father. She wore her blue dress. Eve had put Flora's hair up and fixed it with enough pins to make certain it would stay in place until after the service.

Kade had purchased a new white shirt and black vest. His hair had been trimmed to neatness. He looked so handsome she couldn't take her eyes off him.

Her parents had been relieved when she and Kade returned four days ago to announce they were going to get married.

Her sisters had been overjoyed to think they could help plan a wedding. But Flora and Kade had their own plans.

"We'll exchange vows after the church service."

"That's not a real wedding," Eve said with some dismay.

Flora had been firm. "It's our wedding, and we will do

it our way. Besides, it isn't the wedding that's important. It's the marriage. And we are going to have a great one."

Ma and her sisters had tried to persuade Flora to change her mind, but she wouldn't relent. Nothing about her service would be according to what others thought it should be.

Finally, Ma had lifted her hands in a defeat. "You're getting married. I guess we'll have to be content with that."

They exchanged vows before her pa, her ma, her sisters, and a few close friends of the family.

Then they crossed to the manse where Ma had prepared her usual Sunday dinner. Only this time only the family and the Norwoods were present.

After the meal, Ma set before them a cake specially decorated for the occasion. At Flora's request, it was chocolate.

Pa stood at the end of the table.

Flora squeezed Kade's hand. She had warned him Pa would make a speech. She just hoped it wouldn't be too lengthy.

Pa cleared his throat. "It gives me a great deal of pleasure to see you two married. May God bless your union. May you find happiness together by making each other happy. May the Lord bless you with children. And please come and visit often." He sat down.

Flora's eyes stung at the emotions her pa had revealed.

"Cut the cake," Ma said. "Together."

They did and passed a piece to everyone at the table. The meal over, Flora and Kade rose. Flora hesitated, wondering if she should help with the dishes.

Eve laughed. "Run along. There are lots of us left to share the work."

She needed no more invitation.

Kade had borrowed a buggy for the occasion though Flora had said she didn't mind riding horseback.

"No, I want this event to be different, so we won't ever forget it."

And so, she had agreed. The truth was, she would likely have agreed to anything he wanted simply because she was so happy and wanted him to be equally happy.

Partway to the ranch, he stopped.

"What is it?"

"I want to give you something."

"Kade, you have already given me so much."

He jumped from the buggy, pulled out his pocketknife, cut the stems of a dozen yellow buffalo beans, and handed her the bouquet. "I may not be able to give you diamonds and fancy things, but I can give you flowers that nature provides."

"I'd sooner have that any day than diamonds." She pocketed the pins from her hair and let it fall free.

He tugged at a strand of her hair. "I love your hair down."

"Good, because no matter what I do, it's always down before the day is over."

He held her hand as they drove up to his house. "Wait," he said when she began to climb down. He ran to her side and lifted her into his arms.

He carried her to the house, kicked open the door, and set her on her feet inside the kitchen.

"Welcome home, Mrs. Thomas."

She might have said something in reply, but he kissed her in a way that left her breathless.

Home, a resting place for her heart and a love to cherish.

It was more than she could ever have dreamed of.

DEAR READER

Thank you for reading LOVING A REBEL.

I often choose books based on reviews. If you liked this book or have comments would you please go to Amazon and leave a review so others can find it?

If you've enjoyed this story, and would like to read more of Linda's books, you can learn more about upcoming releases by signing up for her newsletter. You will also be able to download a free book, *Cowboy to the Rescue*. Click here to sign up.

Connect with Linda online:
Website | Facebook | Join my email newsletter

ALSO BY LINDA FORD

Second-Chance Bride

Reluctant Bride

Prairie Brides series

Lizzie

Maryelle

Irene

Grace

Wild Rose Country

Crane's Bride

Hannah's Dream

Chastity's Angel

Cowboy Bodyguard

Made in the USA
Las Vegas, NV
23 October 2022